# Rescuing Emma

## MICHELE E. GWYNN

An M.E. Gwynn Publication

# Introduction

Rescuing Emma was originally written in the Special Forces: Operation Alpha World of New York Times, USA Today, and Wall Street Journal Bestselling Author Susan Stoker in 2018. The origin story contained references to characters created by Susan Stoker. It has now been re-edited/remastered outside of Susan's world in 2023 with a new SEAL Team created by Bestselling Author Michele E. Gwynn as the point of contact team for Outlaw's Green Berets. In addition, Rescuing Emma (and the entire series) contains new bonus scenes not previously published and added for the fans of this series as a "Thank You" for all the support and love.

Cover by Emeegee Graphics
Editing: M.E. Gwynn
Copyright © 2018 All Rights Reserved

Special thanks to Lillian Maddocks-Cummings for participating in the contest on my Facebook fan page to name my hero.

# Contents

# Chapter 1

C aptain Nathan James Oliver gave the signal to halt, then dropped low. The five men at his back reacted fast, falling back against the crumbling stone wall of the tall building on their right. Each one maintained formation, guns aimed forward, all except for Hank 'Hollywood' Jimenez who brought up the rear. His job was to protect their 'six' and he took that job seriously.

"What do you see, Outlaw?" Ghost whispered. He addressed his captain by his code name carefully peering over his leader's shoulder. Ghost resembled his code name. Diagnosed at birth with a mild form of albinism, his blond hair, pale skin, and light blue eyes made Allen Williamson the target of bullies all his life back home in Washington state. He'd finally found the brotherhood every man needed when he joined the army. His sharp mind and quick thinking led to advancement, and his hard work led to special forces training. Green Berets recruited only the best of the best into the fold.

Nate glanced back at his second-in-command. "Movement at ten o'clock, north side of the street, on the balcony." He turned back, focusing his night-vision goggles on that spot.

Ghost located the second-floor balcony and saw the barrel of a rifle extending just over the ledge. A potted plant sitting on the rail hid the gunman's face, but the barrel moved slowly, steadily, right and then left. The guard was surveilling the street below, probably using an infrared scope on the weapon with which to see into the night.

The street was narrow and cobbled, and stretched perpendicular to one of Prague's main roads. It extended into a defunct neighborhood of crowded pre-WWII buildings more in need of tearing down than repair. Their crumbling exteriors were beyond help and yet people still lived in them because they had nowhere else to go.

Their Special Operations Group, or SOG, had been called in early yesterday morning. An American diplomat's daughter had been kidnapped from an international school in London. The diplomat, Ambassador Robert Rand, had recently presented new policy from the White House to tighten sanctions on Qatar for human rights violations. The violations came through a small terrorist group, Black Jihad, led by Mohammed al-Waleed. Black Jihad kidnapped five French scientists with the CDC visiting the country to study an outbreak of meningitis in the region. Accusing the west of deliberately causing the outbreak in order to commit genocide on their people, negotiations broke down after Black Jihad beheaded the first scientist, a woman named Lorraine Bujois.

The immediate global outrage sparked public outcry for swift retaliation, but the response by the French president, at least publicly, was subdued. The truth was the negotiations were just a stall tactic until French Special Forces, coordinating with American and British Intelligence, could pin down the location of the hostages and run a rescue operation. They had help from an insider, a Qatarian asset released from jail a year prior. His release came with strings. French authorities coerced Jamal Almasi into collaborating. He was nineteen years old and had been forced into joining Black Jihad under threat of death to his family. The French government used that information against Almasi while simultaneously implying it was also a possible way out—if he worked for them. They allowed his younger sister to enter France under a student visa and enrolled her in university. With his little sister under the eyes of French Intelligence and his mother and father still stuck inside an impoverished village far from the more modern city of Doha, he was caught between a literal rock and a hard place, forced to comply, and terrified Black Jihad would discover his betrayal. His fear made him cautious, and his caution paid off in information passed on to French Intelligence.

Nate's SOG had been part of that mission slipping into Qatar with the reluctant cooperation of the Qatari government who buckled under threat of severe sanctions to include ending economic aid. The remaining four scientists were found, bound and gagged, inside a sewage tank on the training ground of Black Jihad's compound located thirty-seven kilometers northwest of the coastal city of Doha. They weren't expecting the cavalry, a mistake on their part, and a brief, fatal firefight ensued. In the end, sixteen under-armed over-confident terrorists met their maker, and except for one gunshot wound in the leg of one of their French counterparts, the good guys and the remaining hostages all made it out alive. As close quarter battles went, it was a rousing success.

They'd no sooner spent a week back on base before Black Jihad, learning from their own miscalculations, and angry at the betrayal of Qatar, who they suspected aided the western allies against them, struck once again, this time kidnapping a high-profile target, the seven-year-old daughter of an American ambassador. Since Nate's group was familiar with how and where Black Jihad operated, they were sent back in, this time following their trail to Prague in the Czech Republic—information provided by the informant, Jamal Almasi. They managed to stay on the heels of the kidnappers, and now they were hunkered down against a wall, in the middle of the night, in an impoverished neighborhood inside Eastern Europe.

"I only see one weapon, but there's sure to be more guards on the first floor," Ghost offered, staring hard at the three-story apartment building.

"They've most certainly fortified themselves this time." Nate glanced back. "Skyscraper, take the rear of the building. Check for ways in."

Marcus Dubose, an engineer from Baton Rouge, Louisiana, kept his 6'6" frame low. His ebony skin blended into the night offering him natural camouflage on top of his long-sleeved black jacket, camo pants, and black knit skull cap.

"Roger that," he answered, moving fast in the shadows and slipping around the back of the crumbling brick wall.

"Eastwood." Nate addressed his weapons specialist, Harold Tyler. The big man with a reddish beard often went by 'Dirty Harry', but in combat, it was too much of a mouthful, so his code name had been shortened to Eastwood. "Get into position and find out how many are inside and what kind of weapons we're looking at."

Eastwood nodded, immediately pulling out his thermal imaging binoculars, and hanging them around his neck. He moved past Outlaw and Ghost, sinking low and using the cars parked along the street in front of him as cover.

Behind Nate, Hollywood and Doc, aka Jason Gordon, waited.

"If they've harmed that little girl, I'm going to send those bastards straight to hell with my bare hands," Nate muttered.

"And we'll help you," Hollywood added.

Doc grunted. "Let's hope I don't have to turn my back on the Hippocratic oath." He heard Hollywood snort. "Shut up, Hollywood. I know I never actually took the Hippocratic oath. I'm being facetious," he said, tossing a quick glance in Hollywood's direction. "Look it up. It starts with an F. As in..." Doc flipped the man the bird.

Nate swallowed hard, his teeth grinding with tension. Penelope Rand was inside, scared to death, in the hands of vicious murderers. He'd seen this scenario played out too many times, but this was the first time for him that it involved a child. Knowing the worst in men, seeing the cruelty, the brutality, the sheer psychopathy they could inflict on humans had him feeling anxious and he didn't like it. He knew what it was like to lose a child and he'd be damned if he'd let it happen to anyone else if he could help it.

Nate had always been the calm one, the patient one, but he knew every moment that passed was one in which that child would never be able to recover. The sooner they got her out of there, the better. His hand strayed to the black canvas bag clipped to his belt. Inside was a small fuzzy pink teddy bear. Ambassador Rand insisted that Captain Oliver take it with him to give to Penelope when he found her. Their conversation replayed in his mind.

*"It's her favorite bear. His name is Grover. I gave it to her when she was three and she's slept with him every night since. Give it to her so she knows her daddy sent you. Please!" The desperation in the man's eyes and the fear on his wife's face wrenched his heart. Promising to bring her home, Nate took the teddy bear.*

"Six, come in." Skyscraper's voice came over their earpieces.

"Six here, come back." Nate replied, acknowledging the code. In every operating unit, the commanding officer was referred to over the radio as 'six.'

"There are two back doors. One is locked from the inside. It's located on the far north end. The second is south, near you, and propped open. I found one gunman at that location. He's neutralized."

Hollywood grinned. "My man," he whispered.

Nate nodded to himself. "Good work, Sky. Eastwood, what're the numbers?" He addressed his man now hidden behind a parked car across the street from the apartment building over the two-way radio.

"One family in the eastern, first floor flat. A male, a female, and two children in a back room, all prone. Probably sleeping. Two males with rifles walking the hallway of the first floor as well. A third near the back, southwest door is down, unmoving. Thanks, Sky. Second floor, no families, but four guards with what appear to be Kalashnikovs, and one at the balcony. There's a small room in the middle flat, streetside, where one of the four guards is sitting. There's a child on the floor next to him, unmoving. Third floor is vacant except for the rats, and there is one shooter on the roof, southwest corner, appears to be...sleeping? His hands have slipped from the weapon and he's not moving. Deep, even breathing. Amateur," he added.

"Okay," Nate calculated quickly, and gave the orders. "Eastwood, be our eyes."

"Copy that," he said.

Nate addressed Ghost, Doc, and Hollywood. "You three follow me. We'll meet up with Sky at the southern back door. Stay tight." He moved, staying low, and keeping on the blind side of the second-floor sniper.

When they reached their destination, Skyscraper was waiting for them.

"You lead," he told Skyscraper. "We'll take out the two guards on the first floor, and then proceed to the second floor. Eastwood, where are they now?" Nate asked over the com link.

"Tweedle Dee and Tweedle Dum are leaning up against the north hall wall having a smoke. If you come in low, you can take them out before they even see you round the corner."

Nate nodded and reached forward to grip Skyscraper's shoulder once. The man moved forward, quickly stepping over the prone body of the guard he'd taken down earlier. A long gash across his throat showed clearly the man never had a chance to raise the alarm.

Ghost, Doc, and Hollywood followed in the stack. Once inside, the close quarter battle would intensify becoming far more dangerous. Each man needed to stay sharp.

Skyscraper arrived at the corner that turned into the main hallway and stopped. Nate halted behind him. He could smell the burning tobacco mixed with the stale scents of mold and decay. Voices, low and speaking in Arabic, reached their ears.

With a nod to his captain, Skyscraper double-checked the silencer on his Glock 9-millimeter. In order to make it through to the second floor undetected, he would need to drop the two hall guards quietly.

Skyscraper eased down and cautiously peeked his head around the corner. The muted lighting from the pre-WWII wall sconces cast shadows down the narrow hall. The building's age was to their advantage. He took aim and fired.

Four short bursts found their targets before the guards could raise their weapons. The first went sliding down the wall, his hand-rolled cigarette falling from his lips and landing on the old carpet at his feet. The second guard, who was leaning on the wall, tried to rise to a full stand and aim his weapon when two bullets slammed into his body; one in the forehead, the second in his chest. He dropped to his knees and fell forward onto the burning butt snuffing out the ember.

"Targets neutralized," said Skyscraper. He rose to his feet, waiting for the hand signal on his shoulder.

Nate reached forward, squeezing once. The men at his back did the same. The stack moved into the hall, down past the dead terrorists, to the staircase. "Eastwood, what's the second-floor situation?" Nate whispered, releasing his com switch and waiting for feedback in his earpiece.

"Movement. One of the hall guards is moving to the stairwell."

"Shit," Doc whispered.

"He's going up," Eastwood continued.

"Keep me updated," Nate said before touching Skyscraper's shoulder.

They ascended the old wooden stairs, exercising care and stepping into each other's footsteps to avoid the creaks and groans of the worn treads. The door on the second-floor landing stood ajar, a brick holding it open.

"There's a fire escape to the right and two gunmen to the left; one facing south and the other coming towards your location. The third is still in the flat to your left and the fourth is making his way to the roof. He's going to find Rip Van Terrorist any moment now. You need to hurry," Eastwood urged.

"Copy that." Nate turned to Ghost. "Sky gets the first guard, I'll drop the south-facing target, and you and Doc take the guard inside the flat. Hollywood, you keep an eye on this stairwell. We may need to fight our way out."

"Yes, sir," he replied. Ghost and Doc nodded.

"3...2...1...move!" On Nate's mark, the unit sprang into action, executing the plan.

A tall, bearded terrorist wearing an army-green jacket and a red checkered keffiyeh on his head stopped cold as they emerged from the stairwell. He just managed to get out a short string of words before Skyscraper put two bullets in his head. The second gunman behind him turned. Nate stepped around Skyscraper firing off three quick shots from his own Glock. The silencer muted the sounds of the bullets but couldn't stop the thunk of a body falling to the floor.

"The inside guard is on his feet, fellas." Eastwood's voice came across the com link. He watched through the thermal imaging binoculars as the hazy red figure lifted a device to his face. "He's alerting the rooftop. Repeat, he's alerting the rooftop."

"They know we're here, boys." Nate holstered the Glock and swung his SOPMOD M4 rifle in hand. "Time to make some noise. Aim high. Don't put the girl in any danger."

"Copy!" Ghost nodded to Doc and then, with one kick, busted in the door to the flat, swinging it wide.

Doc sighted the inside guard and sent him reeling in a short burst of fire. Nate ran in behind them and located the girl. Penelope Rand was curled into a ball on a dirty mattress in the corner of

the room. Tear tracks streaked her cheeks. She wasn't crying now, but her blue eyes were wide with shock. Rage and concern flooded him, and Nate went to her, dropping to his knees and pulling the black bandana down off his face.

"Penelope, I'm Captain Oliver, a friend of your dad's. He sent me to get you." He pulled out the pink fuzzy bear from the bag clipped to his belt showing it to her. "I brought Grover to help."

The girl's eyes locked onto the toy. Shock gave way to tears as she began to cry. "I want my mommy and daddy," she whimpered.

"I'm taking you to them. These are my men. Now, I need you to put your arms around my neck and hold on tight, okay?" Nate opened his arms, and the girl ran to him, clinging with all her might.

He locked one arm around her and whispered, "Close your eyes, sweetie, and don't open them until I tell you to, alright? We're getting out of here." He stood and headed back into the hall.

"We've confiscated their phones," Skyscraper said, indicating a clear plastic bag with three cellphones inside. "Got their pictures too so command can identify them. This one's just a kid, for God's sake." He pointed at the dead young man lying on the floor who'd been guarding the little girl. He couldn't have been much more than seventeen.

"Al-Waleed isn't among them," Nate said, looking at the faces of the dead.

"Jihadis coming your way, Six." Eastwood warned.

"Copy that," said Nate. "Do we have time to get back down the stairs?"

"No. Either shoot your way out or take the fire escape," he said.

"Damn." Nate locked eyes with Ghost who, without needing to hear the words, knew Outlaw had already decided the safest route out was down the fire escape. It was for the girl's own safety. Otherwise, they wouldn't hesitate to take on the remaining two terrorists.

"Uh, Six?" Eastwood's voice came over the com link once again. "There's a jeep coming up the road." Everyone froze. Eastwood whispered, "And they're parking in front of the building. There's one, two, three more coming through the front door, and the family on the first floor is starting to move. You got company, son." He picked up his night vision goggles training them on the three exiting the jeep. "Son of a bitch! It's al-Waleed."

Nate cursed under his breath. "Fire escape, now!"

Ghost, Doc, and Skyscraper reached the window first. Skyscraper threw the locks and lifted the pane. He locked it into place. Ghost and Doc slipped through to the rickety metal landing. They released the ladder. The screech of rusted metal as it rolled down unused tracks sounded loud enough to wake the dead.

"You first, Doc. I don't think that platform will hold all of us at once." Nate sent Doc down. Behind them, Hollywood stood next to Outlaw, his M4 trained on the door to the stairwell. He could hear the booted footsteps coming their way.

"Outlaw?"

"Drop anyone who comes through, Hollywood."

Eastwood chimed in over the com. "The family inside just let al-Waleed in. They're in the hall. The man from the downstairs flat is communicating via walkie-talkie to the other two about to land on your floor."

Hollywood tensed. The door swung wide, and a hail of bullets flew. Skyscraper countered on Hollywood's left, dropping low and taking the first gunman out at the knees. The terrorist behind him held back, taking cover behind the doorway.

"Ghost, get down that ladder!" Nate shouted. As soon as Ghost began his descent, Nate slipped through the window, clutching Penelope to him. "Don't be afraid, Penelope. I've got you. Your mom and dad are waiting for you. I promise you're going to see them." His heart pounded, and he prayed he would be able to keep that promise.

Gunfire filled their ears.

"Two men are coming out the front, Six. They're heading your way." Eastwood relayed the play by play.

On the ground, Doc and Ghost got into position to defend their location. Nate looked down at his men. It was a twenty-foot drop from the landing. With the child in his arms, his hands weren't free to climb down or shoot. Time for a change of position.

Squatting down, Nate set Penelope on her feet. He gripped her small shoulders and spoke gently. "I need you to climb onto my back, sweetie, and wrap your arms around my neck. Whatever you do, don't let go, okay?" He turned, reaching back and pointing. "Up you go, as fast as you can. And keep your eyes closed!"

The fear on the girl's face did not stop her from listening to Nate. She scrambled up, wrapping herself tight and clinging for dear life. "Good girl, Penelope. We're going down the ladder now. If you feel yourself starting to slip, just say so and I'll stop and pull you back up, okay?"

"Okay," she whispered. Rapid fire gunshots inside the building startled the child who whimpered.

"It's going to be okay." Nate patted her hands which were locked around his neck, practically choking him. He was proud of her fortitude and in awe she'd managed not to scream. She was a brave girl. She reminded him of Jessica...and Charlie—but he couldn't think about that now.

He turned and gripped the railing, descending the narrow, rusted-out ladder. Above him, Skyscraper and Hollywood held one terrorist at bay. Below, Ghost and Doc engaged the two that came into view from the corner of the crumbling brick walls. Nate's heart seized in his chest. He was used to bullets and could deal with it if one struck him, but the idea of Penelope getting caught in the crossfire had him in a near-panic to get to cover quickly.

Doc drew near, putting himself between any incoming bullets and the child on Nate's back as his captain jumped the last foot off the ladder.

Immediately, Nate turned, swinging his M4 in hand. He touched the com button at his shoulder. "Hollywood, send that bastard to hell."

A static voice answered. "With pleasure."

Above, Skyscraper oozed through the window out onto the landing. Hollywood's leg came through and he was halfway out when Skyscraper dropped down the ladder in one smooth move holding the rails while digging the heels of his boots into the lower, outside railings.

Behind him, Hollywood shouted, "Fire in the hole!" and leaping over the rail, jumped twenty feet to the ground, landing in a practiced roll before covering his head. Skyscraper ducked as did Ghost and Doc. Nate had moved as far from the building as possible pulling Penelope around and into his arms as he hit the dirt, covering her with his body. A loud explosion split the night. Debris rained down; bits of wood, brick, and glass—all potential deadly projectiles.

The two terrorists near the front of the building, who'd been shooting at them, were blown back abruptly. With ears ringing, Nate's men got up, preparing to run for it. They had a two-block sprint ahead of them to the truck they'd left parked on a residential street. It was on the corner near the main road that would lead them out of Prague. Unfortunately, the two terrorists had also recovered. Shots fired anew.

Ghost and Skyscraper took point with Ghost shouting over his shoulder. "Outlaw, take her around back to the other side. We got these two!"

Nate nodded, tapping Hollywood and Doc as he passed. "You two with me." They immediately flanked him with Doc in front on point and Hollywood securing their back. Moving fast, they stepped over and around fallen blocks of brick and metal from the fire escape to the backside of the building where they'd initially entered. Working their way south, they cleared the corner coming around to the street. All around them, windows were lighting up as curious neighbors tried to catch a peek at what was going on.

The gunfight continued. Nate, Doc, and Hollywood reached the street, running across and ducking behind a parked car. Nate lowered Penelope to the concrete, running his hands down her arms and legs, checking for wounds.

"You okay? Any pain anywhere?"

She shook her head. "No. But my ears are ringing."

Nate cupped the sides of her head. "That'll go away. But you can hear me, right?"

"Yes," she nodded.

Relief flooded him. The girl was unharmed and responding well, all considered. "I need you to go with my friend here. His name is Doc. He's a really nice guy. He's going to take you to the truck. I'll be right behind you, too, so don't worry." He looked over her shoulder at Doc. "Get her to the truck, get it running. I'm gonna help get Skyscraper and Ghost free of that ambush. Hollywood, protect their backs."

"Always, Outlaw," he answered.

Penelope looked at Doc who smiled at her, his dimples deepening, a favorite trait of the ladies in his life. The girl smiled back and tentatively reached up, sticking the tip of her finger into one.

"And another one falls," chuckled Hollywood, shaking his head. "Young, old. Doesn't matter. The girls love the dimples, Doc." He shook his head.

Doc snorted. "Blame my mama. She gave 'em to me. And by the way," he said to Penelope, "my given name is Jason."

"I like Doc," she said.

"Then Doc it is, missy. You ready?" He held out his arms. "We're gonna need to go fast so that means I'll have to carry you."

She stepped into his arms. "Okay, Doc."

"Okay, then. Let's roll." He lifted her and holding her close, took off running. Hollywood followed, protecting their back.

Nate watched them go and then turned, staying low and moving fast up the street. He found Eastwood stationed behind an old green Volkswagon. "It's time we rescue those two before the entire neighborhood and local police are on us. Ready?"

Eastwood grinned, lifting his rifle, cocked and locked. "About time. I was getting a little bored over here just watching like some kind of pervert."

"I thought you liked to watch," Nate chuckled, M4 aimed as they crossed the road coming up behind the two Black Jihad terrorists.

"You ain't pretty enough for my tastes."

"That hurt."

Nate squeezed the trigger and the first man fell forward, surprise forever frozen on his face. The second man turned halfway before Eastwood dropped him.

Ghost and Skyscraper quickly joined them.

"What took you so long?" Ghost asked.

Nate grinned. "You're welcome. Now let's get the hell out of here before we have to explain to the local authorities just what we're doing in Prague."

As they took off, Nate noticed Eastwood looking towards the front of the building. "What is it?"

He shook his head. "Al-Waleed. None of these guys we dropped was him. He's still in there."

Nate tensed. He wanted to get the bastard, but there was no time, and they needed to get Penelope Rand out. That was their mission. A snatch and grab rescue operation, not a seek and destroy. Still, it grated. The man had kidnapped a child. He'd also ordered a woman beheaded, a fate he knew might have been

Penelope's had they not found her—or worse. He was a monster and monsters needed to be put down. Al-Waleed would elude them again as he'd been doing for the past year, crossing the unchecked borders in eastern and western Europe. Once upon a time, he'd been all for open borders, but after years of watching terrorists come and go as they please, setting up cells in cities and blowing up innocent civilians with IEDs, he'd long since decided that tight, heavily restricted borders were the answer to help keep the menace of these religious extremists in check.

"Dammit, there's nothing we can do right now, Eastwood." He stared hard at the darkened doorway wishing the man would show himself for one moment. That's all it would take to put a bullet in his skull. A siren in the distance pulled Nate back to the moment.

"We gotta go, Outlaw," Ghost grabbed his arm.

Shrugging off his second-in-command, Nate turned. His men fell in line behind him, and the stack moved with precision in the shadows to the waiting truck.

# Chapter 2

Emma Jane Lewis typed a quick email, attached the article she'd been working on, and hit send. "There, all done."

"It's about time," Becky O'Hare exclaimed. "Happy hour waits for no man, or woman! Now, put this on and let's get moving. Joely and Dina are chomping at the bit to get this party started.

Emma glanced up and took note of the slinky hot-pink dress Becky held up. It had spaghetti straps at the shoulders and looked more like a tunic than a dress. The silky material would show every single lump and bump on her body.

"No way! I'm not wearing that," Emma protested. "I'll look like a hooker!"

Becky pooh-poohed her. "Good. Maybe you'll catch a big, hunky man! It's your birthday, after all, and it's been too long since you last dated anyone. Come on." She held up the dress, shaking it at her friend impatiently.

Emma bit her lip. "I can't believe you wenches dragged me all the way to London and now you want to dress me up like a prostitute. You know I don't wear stuff like this, Becky. I'm going to regret this. I just know it!" She closed her laptop and stood, taking the hot-pink man-trap of a dress from Becky's hands.

"Go on, try it on. It's my present to you," her friend giggled.

"Can I at least wear my Doc Martin's with it," Emma asked, thinking to punk it up a bit and save her toes from the silver heels dangling off Becky's other hand.

"Good God, no! I know you love your comfort wear, Emma, but tonight, you're dressing like a proper, sexy, thirty-year-old woman, not a Sid and Nancy reject. Go!" Becky pointed to the bathroom and handed over the shoes.

Emma threw her the stink-eye and slipped into the bathroom. Her friends had booked suites at the Corinthia Hotel in central London days ago as a surprise. It was her first trip across the pond, one for which she'd been practically kidnapped. Even her boss, Derek Riley, had cooperated by clearing her schedule and forcing Emma to take three days off so she could have a weekend getaway to celebrate her thirtieth birthday.

With the promise to complete her latest exposé on the growing standoff between political parties on immigration, she'd packed her bag, grabbed her passport, and allowed her posse of pals to whisk her off to the airport for an overnight flight to London. They'd arrived in the early hours of the morning, exhausted, but excited. With check-in not until the afternoon, they'd left their baggage with the front desk and gone exploring. Big Ben followed breakfast and then it was off to Picadilly Circus, a two-hour bus tour, and back to the hotel where Emma slept over an hour before finishing her article. Becky slept on in the next bed, snoring loudly, her red curls spread out across the pillow. Emma still felt exhausted, but she had a deadline. Summarizing the points on easing the pathway to citizenship and emphasizing that America was not only built by immigrants but was greater for their cultural contributions because they made the economy stronger, she smiled.

Becky rolled over, rubbing sleep from her eyes, and looked at Emma. "I'm getting up and we're going to get gussied up, missy. Hurry and finish because after that, no more work until Tuesday!"

"Yeah, yeah," Emma replied.

Now, here she was standing on the cool tile floor in a hot-pink, silky shirt. There was no other word for it. If she bent over too far, her backside would be on display to Queen and country.

"Becky, my ass is hanging out!"

Becky poked her head in, looking down. Snorting, she said, "then you better put on your prettiest panties. Show that sweet tush off. With any luck, some gorgeous Mark Darcy-type will be tearing them off with his teeth later."

Emma made a face. "Becky! Mark Darcy types don't tear panties off with their teeth. They bow respectfully and ask if they can kindly remove them." She readjusted the neckline, tucking her breasts in.

A loud peel of laughter rang out. Becky ran up behind her, grabbing the hem and lifting the dress before performing an awkward curtsy. "Pardon me, madame, but may I please rid you of those drawers so that I might poke you repeatedly with my magnificent cock?"

Emma swatted her friend's hands. "That is the worst British accent I've ever heard."

Becky raised a dubious eyebrow. "Maybe, but when Mark Darcy asks, you'll change your tune."

"Only if he's nice, educated, and not some 'roided up muscle-head."

"I don't know what you have against muscles. Personally, I love a strong man." Becky moved around her, shedding her clothes as she walked into the shower, turning it on.

"I just prefer brains over brawn. That's all. And strong doesn't have to mean bulging biceps and other...um...bulges. It can also mean strength of character and having compassion." Emma curled her lip in disapproval as she looked at herself in the mirror, turning left and then right, sucking in her stomach. Her brown wavy shoulder-length hair framed an oval face with big brown eyes made larger by dark-rimmed glasses. At five-foot-two, she was shorter than most women. She made up for it by wearing heels and trendy platforms as often as possible, but she preferred her Doc Martin's when not representing the paper. Those, and jeans and concert t-shirts. She was a nerd at heart, and, at the moment, she was sure Mark Darcy types went for delicate females, not glasses-wearing writers.

"Those things aren't mutually exclusive. Still, you never have seemed to care for the type, but I'm telling you, Em," Becky poked her head around the shower curtain, "there's a lot to be said about those 'other' bulges."

"Just hurry up in there. I need a hot shower if I'm going to make it through this night with you lunatics. And I want cake!" She shimmied out of the dress, hanging it up on the door. Becky began humming as she bathed. Emma smile. She loved her friends, especially Becky who'd been her bestie since high school. Joely and Dina came along in college and the four of them had been inseparable since. The Fab Four, they'd dubbed themselves. Okay, they ripped that moniker off from one of their all-time favorite bands, but they were the female version with loads of pictures to prove it. Vacations, birthdays, holidays, weekend jaunts up to the Finger Lakes wine country of upstate New York, Saturday nights out, and Sunday morning post-hangover brunches. And next, there would be London, the grand celebration of Emma's big 3-0.

She grinned. Maybe she would find her Mr. Darcy here, one who secretly desired a nerd-girl, if only for one wild weekend.

# Chapter 3

E mma fanned herself, eyes closed. "Lordy, it's hot in here. I need another drink."

Becky lifted the napkin from beneath her now-empty gin and tonic, waving it first at herself and then fanning it towards the back of Emma's neck who was holding her hair up. It was a futile attempt to cool them both down. "Make it two, please," she said, glancing around. "Where is our waitress?"

"Couldn't say, but maybe I can solve your problem. What're you ladies having?" Doc approached the redhead, dimples flashing.

Becky dropped the napkin, swallowing hard. Emma noticed the fanning had stopped and turned. She was greeted by a wall. At least, it was as wide as a wall, and solid. Looking up, she found two of the bluest eyes she'd ever seen gazing back at her. They were framed by dark lashes set in a strong, handsome face. She opened her mouth to ask him to back up, then froze. He was frowning.

"What?" Emma looked down in confusion. Embarrassment flooded her cheeks causing her to overheat all over again. Her slip of a dress had slipped down one shoulder revealing the top-most sneak peek at her nipple. "Oh, god," she uttered, quickly pulling the strap back onto her shoulder.

Doc choked back a chuckle while Becky, struggling not to laugh out loud, reached out to pull Emma's hair over her shoulder in a comforting gesture. She leaned over, whispering, "I'm sure he didn't see anything."

"So, I was asking what you ladies were having? I'm Jason, by the way. My friends call me Doc, and this is Nate." He clapped Nate on the back.

"Oh, are you a doctor?" Becky asked, immediately returning her attention to the handsome, brown-eyed, dimpled man.

"Not exactly. I'm a battlefield medic. U.S. Army, ma'am. Nice to find fellow Americans here." Doc poured on the charm. "Who's your friend?" He turned to Emma, smiling.

"My best friend, Emma. It's her birthday." Becky offered, smiling big.

Doc extended his hand. "Nice to meet you, Emma, and happy birthday. Twenty-one?"

Emma bit her lip as she crossed her arms over her chest. Her embarrassment had not yet completely subsided. "Thirty, actually," she replied.

"That cannot be possible," Doc exclaimed. "You don't look a day over twenty-five at most, tiny thing that you are."

Nate rolled his eyes. Emma noticed and frowned.

"Well, I don't think age has much to do with size, and you're just being kind" she said.

"Not at all. I meant it. So, it's a birthday celebration, huh? Well, maybe we can help you make it a party. We have a couple other friends here with us. They're out on the dance floor right now." Doc pointed. "Those two right there. See the guy doing the outdated dance moves? Sad to say, he's with us. So's the tall one but at least he has rhythm."

"No way!" Becky laughed. "They're dancing with our friends. The blonde is Joely and your tall friend is dancing with Dina. How funny!"

"Well, isn't that a happy coincidence?" Doc looked at Nate over his shoulder, winking.

"Are you a battlefield medic too?" Emma asked Nate. She glanced over, studying his face. The handsome man had a couple days growth of beard shadowing his jawline and chin, but it wasn't out of control or messy. Still, she preferred clean-cut and far less brawny men no matter how handsome they were. He caught her watching him and her cheeks flamed again under his scrutiny.

"No," he replied. Nate noted her blushing. She had her arms crossed over her chest in a protective gesture. Half of him wanted to laugh. The other half keenly felt her humiliation. His response probably hadn't helped much, but he couldn't fix that now. He hadn't known quite what to say. It had been a long time since he'd been in the company of women. Saying, "Hey, your nipple is out," didn't seem like a good idea. Reaching out to lift her dress strap would've been too forward. So he'd said nothing, all the while censuring himself for not being able to look away fast enough. His perusal, however, continued. Up close, she was prettier than he'd first thought. Creamy skin, big brown eyes, and just a hint of indentions on her nose that told him she usually wore glasses. He'd always had a thing for women who wore glasses. They implied a certain intelligence, and smart women were damned sexy, not to mention the male fantasy of the sexy librarian.

Emma watched the dance floor, chewing her lip. His short answer left an awkward silence between them. He was obviously not as charming as his friend, nor much of a gentleman. A real gentleman would've apologized at least or shown some kind of effort to look away. The disapproving expression on his face when he'd spied her nearly-naked boob left her feeling embarrassed. She knew she had smallish breasts, but so what? He didn't have to act like he'd seen something repellent. And why did she care anyhow? He didn't know her, and she didn't know him. So what if her boob made an appearance.

"I do know basic life-saving measures."

"What?" Startled out of her reverie, Emma glanced at Nate. He was looking down at her again.

"You asked if I was a medic. I'm not, but I do know basic CPR and such. We're all trained to perform the basics."

"Just not as much as your boss, I guess." Emma held his gaze. "Professional medical personnel aren't put off by the human body, after all."

Nate sputtered, eyebrows shooting up. He was about to set Emma straight on who was boss and tell her he hadn't been 'put off' at all when Doc interrupted.

"To be fair, old Nate here hasn't seen a naked woman in a long time, especially not one as pretty as you." He threw a look of contrived innocence at his captain before returning his attention to the redhead at his side. "And speaking of, I should inform you up front that I offer breast wellness exams free to incredibly gorgeous redheads with freckles, but only if they ask nicely."

Becky giggled, slapping him on his arm. "That's sure assuming a lot, Jason," she said, preferring his given name.

"I'm not one to assume anything, ma'am, just a giving soul who believes in preventative breast care, that's all."

Nate coughed, choking, and, leaning on the rail overlooking the dance floor, buried his face in his hands.

Emma noticed him choking and reached out, concerned, touching his shoulder. It was rock-solid under her hand and the heat from his body caught her by surprise. She pulled away as if burned, dropping her arm to her side.

"Are you okay?" she asked.

Nate felt tingles where her palm had been. It was unexpected, but pleasant. He dropped his hands and looked at Emma, a slow smile spreading across his lips. "Yes. Maybe we should begin again?"

It was the first smile she'd seen on his rugged face. It transformed his features from stern to inviting. It was like night and day, like a punch to the gut that knocked the wind out of her lungs. She swallowed. "Well, I'm not letting you give me a breast exam, if that's what you mean."

Stunned, Nate's smile fell. "That's not what I meant—"

Emma continued talking, rushing on as if he hadn't said a word. "Because I'm not like that, despite the accidental peep show. I mean, I don't usually wear dresses like this. It's just because it's my birthday and Becky bought it for me," she rambled, looking down at the hot pink silky slip of a dress. "Well, the girls whisked me off to London only last night and I've never been to a club in London before. So, really, even though your boss is very charming and I'm sure Becky likes him just fine, and you're probably both good men who serve our country—and thank you for your service—even so, I'm just not that kind of girl," she inhaled, and went quiet.

Nate didn't know what to say. The petite woman with the lovely legs, the glasses indentations on her pert nose, and the prettiest, perkiest breast he'd seen in a long time had just verbally run him down like a runaway freight train. He cleared his throat. "I don't want to give you a breast exam." It was the first thing he could think to say.

"You don't?" Emma wrapped her arms around herself again, stung.

He noticed her body language immediately. He'd stepped into it again. "You just said—what I mean is I would never presume that such an offer was on the table. There's nothing at all wrong with your breasts. They're perfect. Really. And I sound like a complete fool," Nate said, shaking his head and turning back to watch the crowd below.

Emma digested his words. The entire conversation was absurd. Funny, actually, after she replayed it in her head, and a complete disaster. He'd said her breasts were perfect. Why did that matter? It shouldn't matter. He was just a stranger, just some over-muscled soldier...with gorgeous blue eyes and a smile that took her breath away. Now where did that come from, she wondered.

Her lady bits answered, *"From us, you nitwit! We need a little attention and he's hot!"* She made a decision and unfolded her arms, extending her hand. "I'm Emma Lewis."

Nate stared at her slender fingers. When he glanced up, she was smiling at him. The glint in her brown eyes hinted at suppressed laughter. He took her small hand in his large one, engulfing it. The tingles were there again sparking pleasantly against his palm.

He lifted her hand to his lips, placing the lightest kiss on her knuckles. "Captain Nathan James Oliver."

Sucking in a breath, Emma blushed. The heat of his lips on her skin caught her off-guard. She cleared her throat. "Very nice to meet you, Captain."

"Just Nate," he said, smiling.

"Nate," she repeated. They stood staring at each other, unable to break eye contact.

"You ladies want to join our table? We have ringside seats to that disaster of a male exotic dancer," Doc asked, tilting his head towards the table where Ghost and Eastwood sat alone laughing at Hollywood's switch from the robot to Saturday Night Fever moves that looked more like he was having a seizure.

Becky waved her hands in front of her friend's transfixed face breaking the eye contact between her and Nate. "Earth to Emma! What do you say? Shall we join them?"

Nate raised an encouraging eyebrow. "Well? Give me one more chance to make a better impression?"

Emma bit her lip. He really wasn't her type at all. Too rough. Too stern. Too muscled. But her body had other ideas. It was thrumming pleasantly and prodding her to accept. "Okay. One more chance. But you better not be a worse dancer than your friend out there."

"Seriously, he has no hip action at all!" Becky howled.

Doc offered Becky his arm. "Not a problem on my end, Beautiful. Lots of swivel in these hips." He looked at Emma, adding, "Pretty sure Nate has a few smooth moves if you ask him nicely, too."

"Doc!" Nate's eyes narrowed. He'd just earned Emma's acceptance. He didn't need Doc ruining that.

Emma laughed. "I think you're embarrassing him."

"Naw, I'm just pissing him off." Doc tugged Becky's arm, moving quickly to the stairs, laughing all the way.

"Is he?" Emma asked, joining Nate at the top of the stairs.

"Is he what?"

"Pissing you off?" she asked.

"Every chance he gets," Nate said.

"It's terrible to have a boss who's so provoking, isn't it?"

Nate paused, his expression pained. She still thought Doc was his boss. It was time to correct that misinformation. "He's my subordinate, not the other way around."

Emma stumbled on the last step. Nate reached out, catching her, and pulling her close to his side.

"And he talks to you like that?" She stared up at his face.

"All the time."

"And you let him?" Emma felt breathless. The hard-muscled arm around her waist burned her skin beneath the thin layer of hot pink silk. Her stomach flip-flopped like crazy, and tingles swarmed her before settling low inflaming her lady bits.

"Maybe I like sass," he growled. Nate liked the feel of her against his body. He leaned closer.

"Oh," Emma's lips parted. He was moving in, just an inch away. She could smell just a hint of aftershave, something woodsy, earthy, and sexy. It was intoxicating.

"Excuse me!" A tall man dressed like Cher squeezed past them. Cher stopped, glancing back. "Get a room, you two!"

Shocked out of the eye-gooey moment, Emma giggled. It was all too absurd.

"What's so funny," Nate asked, a questioning look settling on his brow.

She noted the change in his eyes. Those blue, blue eyes... Shaking herself, Emma turned her face away from the man. If she continued to stare at him, she might just toss all her standards for men right out the window. Glancing back, she regretted it immediately. He was not an academic, or sensitive type. He was not polished, but rough around the edges, not laid back, but rather, a take charge individual. Nope, Captain Nathan James Oliver wasn't her type at all...so why was her body tingling all over and heating up to a four-alarm fire at his nearness?

She took two steps away moving ahead to give herself some breathing room. The air cooled her skin and she sighed with relief.

"Nothing," she replied, tossing the word over her shoulder.

The shoulder strap slipped loose falling down her arm once again. She reached to pull it back up and her fingers encountered a warm hand... and warm fingers that slid up her bare skin beneath the wayward satin string holding up one half of her minimal excuse of a dress. Her modesty was saved but his touch robbed her of breath. All she could hear above the thumping beat of the music was the clang of fire bells going off from somewhere south of her waistline.

# Chapter 4

E mma stood in the middle of Nate's suite, wringing her hands and wondering how she'd ended up in a strange man's room on her first night in London. She swayed on her feet a bit, feeling the effects of the drinks she'd downed trying to keep up with all the birthday toasts. Nate picked up some clothes that he'd left on the bed and tossed them on the chair in the corner. He turned and looked at Emma.

"Can I get you anything to drink," he asked.

"Just some water if you have it, thanks."

He went to the mini-fridge and pulled out a cold bottle of Evian. Unscrewing the lid, he handed it to her.

Emma took a few sips and looked around the room. "Crazy that we're all in the same hotel, isn't it?"

"A nice coincidence," Nate replied, his lip twitching. He could see she was nervous and found it to be endearing.

"Convenient," she said, then added, "for Becky and Doc, of course." Her best friend and Doc had hit it off right away. It wasn't long before they were making out on the dance floor like unbridled teenagers. When Doc asked where they were all staying, and discovered it was none other than the Corinthia, the two of them couldn't get back to the hotel fast enough. Becky, who'd been broken up with her ex-boyfriend for two months, was more than ready to hop back in the saddle with the smooth-talking, dimpled Doc.

On the way up the elevator, she'd whispered to him, "So about that breast exam..."

Joely and Dina had laughed like loons. Beside them, Hollywood and Skyscraper struggled to stay awake, having imbibed more than their fair share of mixed drinks. Joely was relieved while Dina seemed put out. She and Marcus DuBose had connected and were getting along well. As Hank 'Hollywood' Jimenez began sliding down the wall, the one Nate had introduced as Ghost pulled him back up.

Emma decided right away she wouldn't call him Ghost but would stick to his given name of Allen. It didn't sit right with her to call him by that name. Especially since it appeared he suffered some type of condition, possibly albinism. She hadn't asked. It seemed cruel even though Allen didn't appear to be bothered by it. He was nice, handsome, and an engaging conversationalist. His knowledge of world affairs was impressive. Nate had sat quietly at her side as the two delved into political topics and immigration issues. She noticed Nate hadn't said much, but there were a few times he'd winced, visibly biting his tongue in between the few inciteful tidbits he'd offered. Allen baited him now and again, chuckling when his boss refused to bite. When asked why he wouldn't join in on the conversation,

Allen answered for him. "He's behaving himself for your ben-
efit, Emma." Then he'd leaned over and whispered, "He likes
you."

Those three words made her forget Nate's scanty participa-
tion in their conversation. She hadn't really learned much about
what he thought of these important issues, issues that mattered
to her. But then Allen had shared that Nate liked her and Nate's
blue eyes locked onto hers, causing a riot of warm tingles to run
rampant through her body.

The elevator stopped on her floor and Becky and Doc tumbled out first. Laughing, Becky looked back at Emma. "Give me
a few hours. Nate, take care of our girl!"

"What?" Emma stuttered.

"Yes ma'am," Nate replied, stifling a grin. He glanced down at
Emma. "Don't worry. I have a pull-out couch. You can take the
bed."

Doc heard this and said, "Always the gentleman. Emma, take
pity on the man! He needs a good shagging, as they say here in
Britain."

Joely and Dina stepped out. Seizing the day, Eastwood
jumped off at the last minute with them. He smiled at Joely, taking her hand and caressing her fingers with his. The look he sent
her sizzled with sensuality. Joely licked her lips, offered a saucy
smile, and down the hall they went to her suite. Dina laughed at
them, and then wished Marcus a reluctant good night. The tall
man smiled down at her, eyes half-mast. He was drunk, but not
as drunk as Hollywood who didn't even notice Eastwood had

swooped in and stolen the woman he'd been trying to woo all night.

Dina blew Marcus a kiss. The tall man nearly fell over trying to snatch it out of the air before stumbling upright and holding the invisible kiss near his heart. A goofy smile spread across his face as his eyes shut completely. Dina shook her head and then turned to Nate. "Look, Nate, our girl here needs some good lovin'. It's been far too long—"

"Dina!" Emma squeaked.

"Ain't no shame in being celibate, Emma," Dina said. "The only thing shameful is if you don't grab two handfuls of this gorgeous man and eat him up! At least he's not out of commission like that one, she said, pointing at Marcus before stepping back and laughing as the doors closed on Emma's red face.

Another two floors up and their remaining group exited the elevator. Ghost helped Hollywood to his room. Skyscraper stumbled to his, and Nate and Emma went in the opposite direction to the suite at the end of the hall.

Once inside, she didn't know what to say. So far, she'd sipped water and muttered nonsense about coincidences. Meanwhile, Nate had watched her in his particularly disconcerting way. She had a feeling a lot was going on inside his head, but he didn't say much. As hot as he was, he really didn't need to, and as well as he danced, no other form of communication was needed, at least while on the dance floor. Recalling his hands holding her waist while their hips swayed, his thighs grazing hers, caused heat to suffuse her cheeks. The music led the way, pounding a deep base beat before the DJ transitioned to reggae. It was then, Nate had pulled her closer, sliding his leg between hers and swiveling his hips in a way that sent white-hot desire straight to her core. He'd held her gaze the entire time. It was the most sexual thing she'd ever done in public with clothes on and now he was looking at her again with that same intensity.

"Screw it," Emma mumbled, feeling bold. She set the water bottle down on the dresser, and reaching up, slid the straps of her dress off her shoulders. It fell to the floor in a hot-pink shimmer. She stood naked except for a pair of pink lacy panties and her silver heels.

Nate's sucked in a sharp breath. The heat in his blue eyes blazed as his gaze traveled her body from head to toe taking in all the curves along the way.

Emma began to lose her bravado during his slow perusal. Her hands lifted of their own volition to cover her breasts.

"No." Nate said. He took three steps eliminating the space between them. Reaching out, he gently circled her wrists with his fingers. "Don't do that."

Emma felt like she was standing before a furnace. The fire that sprang to life within her at his nearness threatened to consume her. "Nate, I…"

Hearing her whisper his name brought forth something primitive within him. He wanted her. His inner caveman screamed '*Mine!*' Nate's thumbs caressed the pulse-points on the inside of her wrists. His head dipped low bringing his lips near her ear. "Yes, Emma?"

Nate's breath tickled the strands of hair against her neck setting off sparks.

She took a deep breath and then, before she lost her courage, said, "Kiss me."

Her softly spoken words unlocked a flood of desire. Releasing her arms, he wrapped his own around her waist, pulling her hard against him. His lips captured hers in a searing kiss. It was neither gentle nor slow. It was raw and possessive.

Emma moaned, winding her arms around his neck. Her bare breasts rubbed the material of his shirt meeting the resistance of his muscled chest. The friction caused her nipples to harden painfully. Before she could think, Nate's hand slid up her side. The warmth of his palm covering her naked skin made her sigh and when he massaged her breast, tweaking the hard nub, her knees buckled.

"Oh!"

"You like that?" he growled.

Emma nodded, unable to speak. But her body answered loud and clear, her back arching like a satisfied cat.

A slow smile spread across Nate's lips. "Then tell me, Miss Lewis, what you think of this?"

Emma gasped as Nate bent low, leaning her back over his arm. His mouth captured her nipple, sucking hard before flicking the peak with his tongue.

"Oh, yes. Yes, I like that." Emma's head fell back, and her lips parted as he laved first one breast and then the other with equal intensity. "It's been so long..." she mumbled, then tensed when she realized she'd said that aloud.

"Then let's not keep you waiting." Nate scooped her up in his arms and carried her to the bed.

He laid her down gently. The white-hot passion in his blue eyes promised no quarter. Emma bit her lip, suddenly unsure. She wasn't used to take-charge men, and Nate was definitely taking charge. But it was London, and her birthday. This was the sort of wild, romantic, crazy escapade she was supposed to get up to, right? She might not be a vixen every other day of her life, but here, she could be anything she wanted. She would never see this man again after this weekend, or after tonight for all she knew. That was all the pep talk she needed.

"Nate," she placed a hand on his chest. "Do you have, um, you know..."

He smiled. "Protection?"

Emma let go the breath she was holding. "Yes, do you?"

He nodded towards the nightstand. "We're covered. I've got you, Emma." He caressed her cheek, in awe of the softness of her skin. The look in his eyes shifted. "Damn, you're so beautiful."

Emma's heart melted. In that moment, she felt beautiful, and it was intoxicating. His words made her feel safe, not just protected from pregnancy, but protected from...well, she didn't know what, exactly, but the mood that was so intense before gentled. It was still sizzling-hot, but a trust was born between them.

"I'm sorry, Nate."

His gaze narrowed, confused. "For what?"

"I'm not very good at this. I mean, I don't do this all the time. I'm not a wild and promiscuous woman," she rambled.

Nate stopped her with a kiss. Unlike the first one, this one was soft, sweet, exploratory. He held the sides of her face, fingers sunk deep into her hair, massaging her scalp. Every caress of his lips against hers filled him with a need for more. He wanted to taste every inch of her sweet body, but he was determined to slow down, let her set the pace. Finally, he pulled back and whispered, "I know you don't do this all the time. I know you're not promiscuous, but...you *are* good at this," he nipped her lip, "and if you want to be wild with me, Emma, be wild because I'm sure going to do my damndest to drive you wild, in the best possible way."

They were the right words at the right time.

"Show me!" Emma whispered, nervous and incredibly excited.

Nate didn't need any more encouragement. "Yes, ma'am," he murmured. He moved over her, sitting on his knees and straddling her hips. "Put your hands over your head," he instructed.

When she did, he unbuttoned his shirt and pulled it off. Emma stared at the tanned, muscled chest, his sculpted abs, his strong arms and shoulders. How could she have ever not liked muscles before, she thought. Nate was a magnificent specimen of a man. He rose up and unbuttoned his jeans. In a few quick movements, they were tossed to the floor with his shirt and remaining clothing. Now completely naked, Emma's fear returned. He was big...everywhere!

Nate followed the path of her wide-eyed stare and suppressed a smile. Her reaction to seeing him nude only made it worse as he grew harder before her eyes. When her mouth fell open and she licked her lips, he groaned.

"Let's get you out of those." He glanced down at her pink lace panties.

The scorching intensity in his blue eyes made Emma wet. *How did he do that?*

She watched as he leaned down, and instead of reaching for her panties like she thought he was about to do, he slid his hands up her sides, to her stomach, and straight to her breasts where he gently squeezed and massaged. His head dipped, and he began a slow, practiced assault with his tongue. When his teeth grazed her nipple, she groaned, squirming beneath the heated onslaught.

Nate wanted more. She was sweet, and sexy, and soft. God, it'd been so long since he'd last been with a woman. His body wanted to dive straight in, balls-deep, but he wanted to make this special. Emma wasn't just some bungalow bunny that hung around military bases trying to catch a soldier, she was a lady through and through. And something about that fact drove him crazy with desire, made him want her even more.

He shifted and trailed a line of hot kisses down her belly until he reached the edge of the lace. His fingers eased under the band and tugged them down. The scent of her filled his senses, spurring him on. He pulled the scrap of material off her ankles, and then, holding her knees, spread her legs wide, staring hard.

Emma felt instantly embarrassed, but when she glanced down, he was watching her, lips parted. He held her gaze as his fingers began caressing her inner thighs.

"I'm going to taste you now, Emma."

Searing desire shot through her as the meaning of his words sunk in. His head descended, hands gripping her hips. Emma closed her eyes. It was too much! The first flick of his tongue on her most intimate part sent her reeling. He did not relent. Not for one moment.

"Oh, God!" she moaned.

Nate heard her cries and worked her harder, plunging his tongue deeper, tasting her nectar before flicking her hard nub again. Emma's hips rocked as her thighs clamped tight around his ears. Wanting to take her higher, Nate slid two fingers deep inside, caressing her as he licked.

"Yes! Oh!" Emma jammed the back of her hand against her mouth to keep from crying out. She was getting close to orgasm already and she couldn't believe it. This didn't happen hardly ever with previous lovers. She could usually only reach orgasm quickly when alone, using her vibrator, but here she was shockingly close to losing her mind while this big, gorgeous man found her sensitive spots and showed no mercy.

Nate heard her panting breaths and increased the rhythm. He was so hard, desperate to be inside her, but he wanted her to come first.

"Oh yes. Oh yes. Nate, yesssss." Emma's spasmed as a powerful climax wracked her body. She writhed, her hips bucking as Nate continued, not letting up. Adrenaline rushed through her making her feel languid. As she relaxed, Nate sat up and before she could say 'Hallelujah' he slipped on a condom and slid deep inside her still-throbbing womanhood. She gasped.

Reaching up, Emma grabbed his shoulders and held on for dear life. He thrust deep and laid a searing kiss upon her parted lips. His girth filled her, stretching her tight. Slowly, he swiveled his hips as he kissed her lips. Emma could taste herself on his tongue. Knowing what he'd just done to her and what he was doing now made her lady parts tighten all over again. She rocked forward, feeling his hardness pushing against her walls. Sensations washed over her. She was hot and swollen at her very core as Nate pumped harder, alternating the rhythm.

His arms felt like granite and the cords of muscles in his neck and shoulders stood out in relief as he held himself over her. Emma looked up and found him watching her. She couldn't look away. Each thrust brought them both closer to the edge and she was afraid she'd fall apart into a million pieces if she didn't hold on.

"Wrap your legs around me, Emma," Nate commanded.

Emma did. She locked her ankles around his waist. With her legs high and squeezing tighter, he was able to thrust deeper. The intensity of their eye contact, his erotic command, and powerful strokes sent her tumbling over the cliff once again. This time, Nate joined her.

The world fell away in an explosion of pleasure. Spent, Nate slumped atop her, his head resting in the crook of her neck.

Emma tried to catch her breath even as she held Nate close, caressing his shoulders. She was surprised. Sex had never been this good for her. It was always pleasant, when she'd had it, but outside of private moments, she'd never had orgasms like this. Moments passed in silence. She wondered why it had been so intense between them, and wanted to ask Nate, but a soft snore told her he'd already left the conversation before it could begin. In the silence, her thoughts ran away with her. She'd been incredibly wanton with this man, a man so unlike the academic types she usually dated. They were polite, predictable, and somehow terribly unexciting compared to the man she currently lay beneath. He'd rolled partway off but still had one arm around her waist and one leg flung over hers. The heavy scent of sex hung on the air reminding her of how easily and vigorously she'd fallen into his bed. He'd called her beautiful and meant it. But he didn't know the real Emma. Didn't know the concert t-shirt and glasses wearing nerd nor the card-carrying news junkie and respected journalist that she'd worked so hard to become. No, he knew the sexy, flirty London club girl she'd pretended to be. Would he even like the real Emma? No, she thought. That kind of woman wasn't Nate's type. He was too beautiful, and she was just...Emma.

Feeling overwhelmed, she eased out from beneath him and slipped away to the bathroom, picking up her clothes along the way.

# Chapter 5

I t was quiet down in the lobby, for which she was thankful. She needed to think. Emma sat on a plush white couch near the window admiring the massive globe-shaped crystal chandelier hanging from the ceiling. She didn't know what to do. Spurred on by her own insecurity, she'd left Nate's room in a hurry. A strong need to get away had driven her into dressing quickly and sneaking out, tip-toeing backwards out the door. Once in the hallway she paused. Her room was currently occupied by Becky and Doc, so she couldn't go there. Nate's door was now locked so she couldn't go back in, and she didn't want to. She needed some space between herself and the overpowering sexy force of nature inside. He'd somehow breached all her barriers, knocked down the walls she kept firmly in place against men like him.

Men like him? Emma looked around the corridor, taking in the fancy wallpaper decorating the walls. What about him set off her self-preservation alarm and sent her running out of the room? Sure, Nate had muscles from head to toe but not in a bad way. His were the product of a physical job and not the kind over-done by chronic narcissistic gym monkeys who spent their days staring at themselves in mirrors pumping iron. He didn't blather on about himself like those other types of men either. In fact, he didn't say much at all. He listened instead and only commented when he had something to add to the conversation. He was a pretty good dancer too. He'd been nice, respectful, and wow, a great lover!

Emma couldn't put her finger on a good reason for her apprehension. She just knew she needed a breather. Being near Nate made her breathless and she needed some air. The further she went down the hall, the better she felt. More like herself again. She'd taken the elevator down to the lobby thinking to find a place to kill time. In an hour, she'd text Becky and see if it was safe to come back to her room. Maybe they could remove themselves to Doc's room. It was only fair. Emma found a comfy spot on a soft white couch and sat down. She yawned, reaching up to rub her eyes and stopped. Her contacts needed to come out.

Thankfully, she had the case inside her handbag along with her glasses. Looking around, she noted only the night desk clerk, a tall young man with sandy-colored hair, staring at the computer in front of him, and a dark-haired man with an olive complexion wearing a charcoal-colored suit near the elevator smoking a cigarette. He was watching the desk clerk as he took a long drag and slowly blew the smoke out. Neither paid her any mind.

Emma returned to her task, turning her head away as she plucked out first one and then the other contact. She dropped them into their trays and screwed the lids back on. Instantly, her eyes felt better. She pushed her black-rimmed glasses onto her nose, tucked her contact case inside her handbag, and sat back. She wished she at least had her computer with her, but her phone would have to do for now to keep her entertained.

It was nearly 4:00 a.m. when she texted Becky.

*'Is it safe to come into the room?'*

Three minutes passed before her phone buzzed in reply. *'What? Where are you?'*

Emma's fingers typed. *'In the lobby. Nothing's wrong. Just would really like to crawl into my bed.'*

The phone buzzed. *'Jason left back to his room over an hour ago. What can I say? It was quick. Get up here and I'll fill you in.'*

Emma chuckled. She'd been sitting down in the lobby for an hour when she could have already been asleep. She stood, firing off a quick *'I'll be right there'* before heading to the elevator.

She pressed the button, waiting. The floor bell dinged, and the doors slid open. Emma stepped inside, weary and ready for bed. She turned to press the button for her floor. As the doors slid closed, a hand reached in, stopping them.

"Hold the elevator, please." A man stepped in. It was the same one she'd noticed earlier standing around smoking a cigarette. The scent of tobacco lingered around him.

Emma stepped closer to the control panel pressing the Door Open button. "Sure. What floor?" she asked, hand hovering over the panel.

He looked at her, dark eyes taking in her hot pink dress. "Ten."

The doors slid closed.

# Chapter 6

Nate's head was pounding, which didn't seem right because he didn't remember drinking that much. As the fog of sleep lifted, he realized it wasn't his head pounding, but rather, someone pounding on his door.

He got up and took three steps before remembering he was naked. He called out, "Hold on!" and turned to grab his jeans off the floor. He pulled them on, glancing around. The room was empty. Emma was gone. He hadn't even heard her leave and wondered why she did. It was probably her at the door. He smiled, moving to let her in.

Nate swung the door wide. "What in the world are you doing out here, sweetheart, when you should be in bed with me?" He stopped immediately.

Doc stood on the other side, Becky next to him in tears.

"I take it that means she isn't here with you?" Doc leaned in, looking around Nate's room. "Goddammit," he said, running a hand over his face.

Confused, Nate looked from Doc to Becky. "What is it? What's going on? Where's Emma?"

"That's what we're trying to find out," said Doc.

"She texted me around four and said she was coming back to the room, but she never showed up!" Becky pushed past Nate. She began pacing, looking at the bed, then into the bathroom. "She didn't come back here?"

Nate's heart jumped. "No. But then, I didn't even know she'd left. I just discovered that when you two woke me. Where was she when she texted you?"

Becky held up her cell phone. "She said she was in the lobby." Nate turned heading for the door, but Becky stopped him. "I've already been down there. I talked to the front desk guy. He said he saw her sitting down there but that she'd gone back upstairs. There's no sign of her anywhere. That's when I went to get Jason."

Nate listened to the redhead until she ran out of steam. Tears welled in her eyes again.

"Have you checked with your other two friends?" Surely Emma would've gone to one of them.

At that moment, the two friends in question arrived at his door, Skyscraper and Eastwood right behind them.

"She didn't come to my room or Dina's," Joely stated. "She has to be somewhere here in the hotel. Where else would she be?"

Nate looked at Doc. Experience taught them to recognize signs others would ignore because the alternative was just too horrible to consider. Emma had made it clear she was on her way to her room. She never showed up. Never communicated again over the last four hours with her friends. The desk clerk was the last person to see her. Something happened between the lobby and Emma's floor. They each exchanged a look with Skyscraper and Eastwood, who stood waiting automatically for his orders.

"Eastwood, you come with me. We'll go see the manager on duty. They have security cameras everywhere. Let's check those first." He addressed Becky and Doc next. "Keep calling her cell phone. If she's just somewhere in the hotel asleep, she'll eventually answer, right?" Nate tried to offer some hope to Becky and her friends. Inside, his gut was clenched in a tight knot. He didn't know Emma like they did, but he felt sure she wasn't the type to up and disappear leaving people to worry about her. She was too considerate and kind for that. Why she'd left his room in the first place was a question for another time, however. Still, it seemed all she intended was to return to her own room.

"We can call Rio. He can ping her cell phone," Skyscraper offered.

"Good idea. Do that now and tell him Outlaw said this is a fucking priority and he owes me one," Nate barked before taking a calming breath. Rio was his friend, a fellow soldier and Navy Seal he'd served with on joint missions between the army and navy. His real name was Jesse Taggart, but as his southern drawl gave away, he was from the Lone Star state—specifically, El Paso and the Rio Grande Valley—hence the nickname, Rio. Taggart had taken sniper fire on a mission that put him out of commission for more than six months. His SEAL team expected him to return. Even Rio planned on returning, but that reunion never happened. Without explanation to the rest of the team, Jesse Taggart was reassigned to NAVWAR, one of the six SYSCOM Echelon II organizations within the United States Navy that focuses on communications, intelligence, surveillance, and reconnaissance to solve problems and accomplish missions. But even within that higher command, Taggart was in a league of his own. As in everything he did in life, he excelled. If someone was wanted or missing, the best chance at finding that person was through Rio.

Dina's brow creased. "Who the heck is Outlaw?"

"Me," said Nate.

"What's with these nicknames anyhow," Joely asked, pinning Eastwood with a hard stare.

Eastwood remained uncharacteristically quiet, throwing a quick glance at Nate.

"They're code names," Nate answered. "And that's all you need to know."

"What kind of an answer is that? Who are you guys?" Joely's feathers were ruffled, and Dina moved to stand next to her while wrapping an arm around Becky's shoulders, pulling her close.

Nate ignored her. "Make the call, Sky. Eastwood, you're with me. Doc, stay with the ladies and rouse Hollywood and Ghost."

"We should call the police immediately," said Dina. "We can't waste any more time." The prosecutor in her took over.

Nate pulled on a t-shirt and his boots. He grabbed a shoulder holster from his luggage, strapped it on, and then from a smaller lock box inside the suitcase, withdrew his Sig Sauer 9 mm. He slid a clip in, popped it into the holster and turned to grab a jacket. The three women stared at him, eyes wide.

"Seriously, who the hell are you guys?" Dina demanded.

Skyscraper shook his head at Dina giving her the 'cut it' hand motion, but Nate answered, his voice steely. "We're the goddamned cavalry, Dina. You call the police if you want, but in the meantime, we're," he looked at his men, "going to find Emma because I can tell you this, if she's been taken there isn't a minute to spare."

⟫⟫⟫⟩ ⟨⟨⟨⟨⟨

Rio glanced down at his cell phone. The caller ID revealed a number he hadn't seen in some time. Clicking the green button, he answered. "Hey, hey, good buddy. How the hell are you, Skyscraper?"

A short, deep chuckle was heard on the other end. "I could be better, my friend."

Rio picked up on the serious tone in Marcus Dubose's voice right away. "What is it? Something happen to Outlaw?"

"Naw, man. His lady."

Rio stifled a snort. "Outlaw found himself a woman? No kidding? Well, it's about damned time—"

"We think she may have been abducted," Skyscraper continued. "It's been about four hours since anyone's heard from her. That's a four-hour head-start, man."

Rio leaned forward in his chair. "And why do you think she was taken? Where are you?"

"We're in London, at the Corinthia Hotel. The State Department put us up for the weekend after the PR ceremony for Ambassador Rand."

"I saw that on the news. So, you guys were the team, eh? I kinda figured. Cobra and his crew were just by yesterday preparing to leave on a trans-Atlantic transport tomorrow." Rio referenced his old unit leader, Ian Scott, codename, Cobra, and his former team members, Breaker, Havana, Gator, Dragon, and Hendrix.

Skyscraper didn't confirm Rio's question, but immediately returned to the subject. "Outlaw is checking security cameras with Eastwood now. We should have some information soon. In the meantime, he wants you to trace her cell phone. Her friends have been trying to call, but no answer even though it's still on. It's not going directly to voicemail yet. Her name is Emma Lewis and she's from DC." He rattled off the number to Rio.

"Okay. I'll start there. Call me back as soon as you have more. And Sky?"

"Yeah."

Rio swallowed. "Tell Outlaw..." His words trailed off. He knew the hell Nate had gone through with Jessica. He knew he was the only person Nate had confided in not long after the man's life fell apart. It was in Rio's house one winter evening after sharing a case of cold beer together when the painful story tumbled out of Outlaw's mouth followed by a round of vomiting. The night ended with Rio helping Outlaw into the spare bedroom where he slept it off. "Tell him I'll do everything I can to help him find Emma."

# Chapter 7

"There!" Nate pointed at the screen. The hotel manager, Giles Frobish, had been reluctant at first to cooperate with the rough-looking Americans, that is, until Nate made a call to Ambassador Rand's office. A quick explanation transpired, and he handed off the phone to Mr. Frobish who swallowed hard, replied 'Yes, sir,' twice, and hung up. After that, he'd opened the door to the security office and invited Nate and Eastwood inside.

A wall of monitors sat behind a desk with a series of computers attached. The manager typed in his password and pulled up the footage recorded overnight. The screen revealed Emma stepping off the elevator around 3:00 a.m. She walked to the lobby and sat down on the couch. A second camera aimed at the front desk showed the night clerk and beyond that, the elevators where a man entered the frame from a back hall. He stood near the elevators smoking a cigarette while alternately surveying the front desk and then Emma sitting in the lobby.

Nate swore.

"Goddammit, that's al-Waleed! What the hell is he doing here?" Nate slammed his hand down on the table.

"This can't be a coincidence, Outlaw," said Eastwood. He looked at his leader, jaw clenched. "There's no way he just happens to be here in this hotel."

Mr. Frobish sped the reel up. Emma removed her contacts, put on her glasses, and after a bit, stood, walking to the elevator. Al-Waleed was not there initially while she waited for the elevator car to open. He'd moved out of frame when she was sliding the dark-rimmed glasses onto her face.

Nate's nostrils flared as he watched her step into the elevator and turn, facing out. The doors began sliding closed when al-Waleed rushed forth, sticking his hand through the open space to stop them. They re-opened and he stepped inside. Nate could see Emma smiling as she turned her face to the man. Her mouth was moving, but he couldn't hear her words. The security cameras didn't record sound. It looked like she was asking him which floor because she reached out to push a button. The doors slid closed.

"Where's the footage for her floor?" Eastwood asked the manager.

"Hold on," said Mr. Frobish. He tapped a few keys.

The image for the seventh floor showed the elevators at the same time in which Emma had entered below in the lobby. The doors never opened on that floor, at least, not for another forty minutes when one of the seventh-floor residents left to go down.

"Check all the floors, Frobish. She had to get out on one of them." Nate barked the order, feeling sicker by the minute. He looked at Eastwood. "Something is wrong, Harry." He pulled out his cell phone. "I've gotta get Rio on this. I need this bastard tracked. And we need to inform the General. Al-Waleed's being here means something is going on, means he's been following us all night. Goddammit, if he's hurt Emma, I'm going to kill him."

Eastwood nodded. "I agree, but we don't know yet if he's got Emma."

Nate turned to him. "You're the one who just said this can't be a coincidence, Harry!"

The man held up his hands in surrender. "I know, man. I'm just trying to remain open until we have concrete proof he has her. That's all."

Mr. Frobish interrupted the quarreling men. "You might want to see this."

Nate and Eastwood both looked at the screen.

"It's the basement level, where we keep the laundry." He pointed.

On the screen, the elevator doors opened in the dark corridor. Al-Waleed stepped out backwards pulling an unconscious Emma by her arms, dragging her across the floor. When they cleared the doorway, al-Waleed looked around, grabbed a rolling laundry bin and wheeled it next to her. He bent down, lifted her up, and dropped her onto the dirty laundry. He covered her with a load of towels and sheets and pushed the bin down the darkened hallway out of the camera's range.

"Where does that hall go?" Nate asked, glaring at the screen.

"Out to the loading dock behind the hotel." Mr. Frobish answered, worry written all over his face. "Is this man a terrorist? Did one of my guests just get abducted by a terrorist?" He looked sick.

Nate noticed the man's increasing panic. "He's the leader of Black Jihad, and that information doesn't go beyond this room, Frobish. You are not to speak to anyone about this, not with any of the staff, no one. The Ambassador is on this already and he and Scotland Yard will be here shortly. You show them what you showed us."

"I understand," said Frobish who straightened his tie. The man looked green around the gills. Nate felt the same.

He hit the speed dial on his cell phone. It rang twice before Rio answered.

"Outlaw, tell me you have more information." Rio's voice came over the speaker.

"Al-Waleed has her."

"What? Are you sure?"

Nate paced. "Security footage showed him getting into the elevator with Emma. He knocked her unconscious and secreted her out through the basement. Please tell me you've got something from her cell phone."

Rio heard the pain in his friend's voice. "I do. Cell towers pinged her number at the port in Dover."

"Shit," Nate barked. Thinking hard, he paced. "He's taking her to France. Intelligence on Black Jihad shows they have a cell somewhere outside of Paris. He'd go there. I'm sure of it. And he'll be traveling by car. He can't risk public transportation with a hostage." Nate looked at Eastwood. "Find out what Ferry runs there and where to."

"It's the Calais Ferry," said Mr. Frobish.

Both men looked at him expectantly.

"Well?" Eastwood prompted, his green eyes narrowing.

Frobish cleared his throat. "The Calais Ferry runs several times a day between Dover and Calais. It's about an hour and a half each trip and the trip from here to Dover proper is nearly two hours, give or take traffic."

"Damn. That's his head start right there. We'll need help. Eastwood, inform the guys. We need to go."

***

Emma came to slowly. The first thing she noticed was that her mouth was dry. She tried to lick her lips, but something was in the way. She attempted to remove the barrier, but her hands would not cooperate. Full awareness sunk in as she realized there was tape over her mouth and her hands were tied behind her back. Confused, she opened her eyes, looking around at her surroundings.

She was in the back of a small commercial truck lying on a tarp that smelled like fish. The truck was moving, rocking her back and forth. Emma struggled to sit up which wasn't easy with her hands behind her back. She managed to use her head and shoulder against the side wall to scoot into an upright position. That's when she noticed her ankles were also tied.

Shaking her head to clear away the cobwebs, she searched her memory. The last thing she remembered was standing in the elevator. She was going up to her room. And there was a man in the lift with her, a man with dark hair wearing a dark suit. When he'd entered, he walked to the back of the car leaning against the rail. It wasn't an ideal situation. Women everywhere know not to ride up an elevator with a strange man, but he'd jumped in at the last moment. There wasn't anything she could do but hope he wasn't one of those men for whom women should be afraid. She'd been wrong. A vague memory of a hand coming around from behind covering her mouth and nose teased her thoughts. She'd been drugged. Chloroformed, most likely. Dread filled her gut.

Fuck!

Now she was tied up inside the back of a truck—God knows where—all because she'd run from a man who'd been nothing but kind, sexy, and incredibly giving in bed. All because she didn't know what to think about Nate. He wasn't her usual type. He was a soldier, a beefcake by any woman's standards, and not the collegiate type she was used to. She was a nerd and according to her own messed up thinking, only another nerd would ever be attracted to her, not someone like Nate. But he had been, at least, for the night. And the things he'd done to her body, well, that was pure magic and not like anything she'd ever experienced before. And it scared her.

*Dammit, Emma!* she chastised herself. *You coward. Now look where you are! Nate wasn't scary. This is scary!*

Glancing around for clues, she found none. All she saw was a tackle box. But there might be something inside she could use as a weapon. A hook? A fishing knife maybe? Fighting back panic, she scooted closer to the tackle box, turning her body so she could open it. Fumbling with the latch was hell. Emma could unsnap it, but she needed to be able to lift the lid, and then turn her whole body to look inside. It took several attempts, but finally, she applied enough force to pop it open. Twisting around, she checked the contents.

There were a few hooks with feathers attached. They were sharp enough but trying to pick away at her ties would take forever. Emma glanced at her ankles. They were tied with a thin rope. It stood to reason that was probably the same material that bound her wrists. She returned her focus to the tackle box. The first tray didn't reveal anything more that could help, but there was more storage beneath that tray.

Tears welled in Emma's eyes as she realized she would need to remove the top tray quietly so as not to alert her abductor in the front of the truck. Fear and frustration took hold.

*Shake it off, Lewis!*

Scooting around again, Emma began the process of seeking out the seam between the tray and the box with her fingernail. After several unproductive attempts, she finally slid her nail in.

Now she needed to lift the tray out. Pulling up with her nail, she reached with her second finger to lift. It was excruciatingly slow but the moment she was able to slide all four fingers beneath the tray felt like a victory. She was able to grip it and rotate out and away to set the tray down behind her. Now the internal storage of the box was exposed.

Excitement filled her as her eyes landed on exactly what she needed. A small fishing knife. She maneuvered to grab it and immediately began moving the blade into position to cut through the ropes. It took forever, what with her hands feeling numb and having difficulty gripping the handle. After nearly fifteen to twenty minutes of sawing away, she freed her hands. The relief was instant as the circulation returned. Painful pinpricks suffused her hands as Emma rubbed them together, flexing her fingers. As good as it felt, she couldn't waste any time. She reached down, cutting through the ropes binding her ankles.

She was free from the rope, but still locked inside the back of a moving truck. However, now she had a weapon. This meant she had a chance. All she could do now was wait.

# Chapter 8

The Merlin MK2 chopper flew across the Strait of Dover toward Calais. Nate, Eastwood, and Ghost sat in the back along with Skyscraper, Hollywood, and Doc. Thanks to Ambassador Rand, and cooperation between General Davidson, the French government, and the British Royal Navy, they were now closing the gap between them and al-Waleed. What they still didn't know was where he was headed inside Paris. What they did know was what he was driving—a small white commercial truck with a faded sea bass painted on the side. An agent inside MI5 owed Rio a favor and that gentleman obtained the video feeds from the docks in Dover. As he sat in the queue waiting to drive onto the Ferry, al-Waleed had climbed out once to smoke a cigarette and then went around the back of the truck where he lifted the door a mere few inches peeking inside. It was suspicious behavior, but no one seemed to pay him any mind.

Nate was frustrated. He could not see into the truck, could not see Emma. The only consolation he had was that the terrorist was checking on her which meant she was still alive.

"We'll get her back, Outlaw." Doc patted Nate's shoulder as they all watched the video footage from the link Rio had sent.

As they boarded the chopper, Rio messaged Nate. *I've got the vehicle on satellite. They just landed in Calais and drove off the ferry. I'll keep you informed, but you'll probably catch up to them yourselves in about an hour. I'm sending you a link to the satellite feed. Coordinates are on the screen. ~ Rio'*

Now they were in French airspace about to fly over Calais. Nate's eyes rarely left the screen of his phone. The orange pinging dot moving slowly towards Paris was his lifeline to Emma. It seemed strange that only five hours ago, she'd been in his bed, in his arms, panting his name. As sexy as she was, he'd been far more moved by the moments before and between the passionate highs. Emma was a revelation. She was complex. Shy one moment and then bold the next. Unsure, then confident, and then funny as she laughed at herself for being, in her own words, 'such a dork.' She didn't talk about herself like a lot of people do. She asked personal questions and listened. And she could discuss global political issues like a seasoned pundit. The sexy librarian for sure. She'd made him smile, made him feel comfortable and yet excited as hell. Nate remembered dropping light kisses on her cheeks and her nose, and running his fingertip over the tiny indents from the glasses he still had not seen on her face, not until he'd viewed the hotel's security camera footage. They made her look younger, smaller somehow, but also stronger.

He liked it. He liked her, and now, because of him and the work he did, a murderous terrorist had her, and the clock was ticking. It was Emma's thirtieth birthday, and because of him, it might be her last. Nate couldn't accept that, didn't want to be responsible yet again for the death of an innocent. He shook off that thought and focused.

Ghost tapped his arm. Speaking into the mic in his helmet, he said, "There."

Nate glanced out the window. Ahead, the small truck bumped along A26 just a few miles shy of Saint Omer.

He leaned over, tapping the pilot on his shoulder. The pilot glanced at him and said, "Interpol is coordinating with local police. There's a roadblock two miles up. We have the rear."

Nate nodded and relayed the message to his men. "Get ready. We're coming in the backdoor. Ghost, you're with me. Eastwood, Skyscraper, you take the driver's side and Doc and Hollywood, you take the passenger side. We still don't know if he has anyone else up front or if the truck's wired. We neutralize him first."

"Got it, Outlaw," said Hollywood.

They pulled the bandanas tied around their necks up over their noses disguising their faces. Double checking their weapons, they moved nearer the door of the helicopter. Ahead, the traffic in front of al-Waleed began to slow. There were three vehicles in front of him. As each reached the roadblock they were waved through by a French traffic cop. It all looked routine. The vehicles on the ground could not see the SWAT-style Gendarmerie vehicles parked behind the tree line on the right.

The pilot took the helicopter down as the car in front of al-Waleed's truck was waved through. The policeman stopped the truck, stepping off the road as the Gendarmerie tactical vehicle pulled forward, blocking the road. The small truck slammed on its brakes. The gendarmes swarmed out of the back of the tactical vehicle. Al-Waleed threw the truck in reverse and stopped cold when he saw the chopper landing behind him.

Nate and his men jumped out, running up from behind and shouting in Arabic, "Hands out of the window. Hands out now!" One pair of hands emerged from the passenger side.

"There's two of them! Doc, Hollywood, is it al-Waleed? Confirm." Nate yelled.

"Negative, Outlaw. We have another player." Doc shouted as he and Hollywood closed in, rifles aimed.

"Exit the vehicle slowly or I'll send you to hell," Hollywood commanded the passenger.

A shot rang out from the driver's side, and all hell broke loose. Rapid fire ensued as al-Waleed ran ducking into the woods.

Eastwood and Skyscraper joined the chase as half the Gendarmes pursued. In the cover of the trees, bullets couldn't find their target.

Nate glanced around the other side of the truck. Doc and Hollywood stood over the second terrorist. He lay halfway out of the passenger seat, legs still caught in the truck, bleeding out. They were checking him for an explosive vest.

"Any devices in the cab?" Nate asked, inquiring after a trigger.

Doc pulled the dying man out dumping his body on the asphalt and searched the cab's interior. He leaned back out, "None that I can see."

Nate nodded. He returned to the back of the truck addressing Ghost. "Slowly. We don't know for sure what's inside."

Ghost unlocked the door and inched it up revealing a small space. Nate knelt, looking inside. A sharp knifepoint shot through the opening. Nate fell back, catching himself. "Woah! Emma, is that you?"

"Nate?" Emma's voice frantically replied. "Nate! Get me out of here!"

"It's me, baby. It's me. We're all here."

"Oh my God. Thank God. Get me out!"

"We will. Be patient. Tell me, are there any wires around the door that you can see?"

"No. There's nothing. Just the side vents and a tarp and tackle box that I already raided."

Nate let go the breath he'd been holding. "That's good. Okay, step back."

Ghost and Nate pushed the door up. As soon as she had clearance, Emma launched herself straight into Nate's arms.

He swung Emma around, holding her tight. "Are you okay? Did he hurt you?"

Emma breathed in his scent, letting loose the tears she'd been holding back. "No. I'm okay."

Nate ran his hands over her back and head, checking despite her assurances that she was fine. The tightness in his chest eased with each passing moment. He looked down at her, noticing her glasses for the first time. They were askew, having been bumped aside in his tight embrace. She straightened them automatically. His heart skipped a beat.

"We'll need to interview her." A man in a black suit approached, speaking in a thick French accent. He extended his hand to Nate. "Captain, I'm Pierre Laurent, Interpol."

Nate refused to let Emma go to shake the man's hand. He nodded instead. "I'll make sure she's debriefed. Right now, I'd just like to get her out of here."

Laurent handed Nate a card. "This is my counterpart in London. He'll meet you at the American Embassy. Take her there straightaway while her memory is still fresh."

"What about al-Waleed?" Nate asked.

"Looks like he may have slipped our net," said Laurent, looking over Nate's shoulder.

Nate turned. Skyscraper and Eastwood were walking towards them with two of the Gendarmerie. The disappointment on their faces confirmed Laurent's suspicion.

"No worries, Captain. We'll get him." Laurent pulled out his cell phone and began speaking rapidly as he walked back to his sedan.

Emma remained silent during their exchange, loathe to break contact with Nate's chest. She felt safe in his arms. *Why the hell did I ever run from this*, she thought.

"How did you even find me?" She looked around and then up at Nate, wide-eyed.

"It's what I do," he said.

Emma looked over his shoulder. The rest of his men stood by, smiling at her, all except Eastwood and Skyscraper who appeared angry and frustrated. She wondered if it was because of her or because her kidnapper got away. They stopped pacing and nodded at her. Allen reached out and patted her back.

"Glad you're okay, Emma."

"Thank you, Allen." Emma disengaged from Nate and hugged Ghost.

Nate reclaimed her immediately. "What happened, Emma? Why'd you leave me?"

It was a question she'd been trying to answer herself before everything went south. "I got scared," she said simply.

"Of what? Of me?" Nate's blue eyes searched hers.

"I don't know. I just needed to be alone. I'm so sorry."

"You don't need to apologize, Emma. This wasn't your fault. Al-Waleed did this."

Her eyes popped wide. "As in the leader of Black Jihad?"

"Yes. The one and the same."

"What in the world did he want with me? Was it something I wrote?"

Nate's brow creased. "What do you mean?"

"We need to go, Outlaw," Hollywood interrupted. "The chopper's waiting."

"You're not leaving me?" Emma clutched Nate's arms.

"Not on your life. You're coming with me. I'm not letting you go." He pulled her in closer.

"Good," she whispered, snuggling into his chest.

Nate leaned down, moving in for a kiss.

"Time for that later, Outlaw," Doc chuckled, slapping Nate on the back as he jogged past him, ducking low and jumping into the chopper.

"I've never been in a helicopter before," said Emma, eyeing the military chopper with trepidation.

Nate smiled. "Don't worry. I've got you. I won't let you go the entire ride back." He squeezed her hand.

"Promise?" Emma asked, biting her lip.

Nate's eyes followed the movement and he grinned. "Promise. And Emma?"

"Yes?"

"When we get back, the next set of teeth nibbling that lip are going to be mine," he growled.

Emma's heart pounded in her chest as heat suffused her cheeks. There was no chance to reply. Nate led her to the chopper where he helped her in before climbing up behind her. True to his word, he held her the entire flight back to London.

# Chapter 9

As soon as they arrived back in London, Emma was whisked off for debriefing with American and British Intelligence in a separate room down the hall inside the American Embassy. Nate wanted to go with her, to help her through it all, but was ordered to stay behind. He and his team had their own debriefing to attend with the general.

"The good news is, we were able to contain the situation before it got out into the media." General P.K. Davidson sat at the head of the table in the conference room. "This would've been a damned shitstorm had it leaked."

Nate and his men remained quiet knowing Davidson's mood was precarious. The wrong word and he'd have their heads on a platter for dinner. It was one thing to be sent on a planned mission, but quite another to have a terrorist personally come after a team and then abduct an American citizen.

"Anyone want to tell me how the hell al-Waleed knew where to find you?" The General drummed his fingers on the mahogany table.

Nate and Ghost exchanged a look before Nate spoke. "With all due respect, sir, I don't know. We saw al-Waleed at the house in Prague, as stated in my report, but there is no way he could've identified us. We followed every protocol. Camouflage was ensured with both clothing and paint sticks. Our faces were not revealed. We weren't followed."

Davidson pounded his fist on the tabletop, leaning forward. "Then how in the goddamned Sam Hill did he find you, Captain? How is it he just happened to be in the same hotel in London where we granted your team leave, hmm?"

The team looked at each other, angry, but wondering the same thing.

Nate opened his mouth to reply when Davidson cut him off, stunning him. "And just what the hell are you doing fraternizing with a journalist? Have you lost your damned mind?"

Nate's eyebrows shot up and his mouth opened and closed like a fish caught out of water. "What journalist? I haven't—"

"The girl, Captain!" Davidson roared. "Your little fling who caused this whole damn clusterfuck. A Washington Evening Post reporter who can out your entire team to the world. What the hell were you thinking," The General snorted. "Never mind. I know what you were thinking with, and it surely wasn't your goddamned head!"

"Sir?" Ghost spoke up. "None of us were aware of any reporter."

The General glared at Ghost. A file folder sat before him off to the side. He dragged it over and opened it. Blowing out a steadying breath, he began to read. "Emma Jane Lewis, age thirty as of yesterday, employed for the past three years by the Washington Evening Post. She covers politics under the byline of E.J. Lewis. A bleeding-heart liberal to boot. A graduate of the University of Maryland, Baltimore with a major in communication and a minor in political science. Volunteered with Get Out and Vote community outreach, Meals on Wheels, and the Baltimore animal control services adoption center. She also currently volunteers her time in DC with a multinational women's center that focuses on educating women in countries where it is expressly forbidden to do so." Davidson turned the file around and pushed it at Nate. "Quite the little busybody, your lady, Captain."

Nate looked at the picture inside the file staring back at him. It was Emma. His Emma. The shock of discovering she was the same E.J. Lewis who wrote the articles he read, the ones that, in his opinion, gave away far too much information to terrorists like al-Waleed grated on him and kept him from responding. All he felt in that moment was a sick combination of anger and betrayal. In the middle of that mess was the realization that it might not have been him and his men al-Waleed had been targeting after all. What was it Emma had said when he rescued her? She'd asked if Black Jihad was after her because of something she wrote.

Finally, "General, I don't think al-Waleed even knew we were there. I think he was after Emma."

"What do you mean, Captain?"

"Have you read her articles? Her view favors a more open policy regarding immigration, a pathway to citizenship and integrating into American society."

Davidson sat back, considering. "And how does that not play into the schemes of a terrorist organization? They want that, they want to be able to come and go unhindered. Hell, I'd think he'd send her some damned flowers and chocolates for promoting policy that helps them!"

"Not necessarily," Ghost interrupted. "Black Jihad doesn't want their people to leave. They don't want any westernized influence and anything that makes it easier for refugees to flee into the west would be something they'd seek to stop." He looked at Nate. "I think you're right. He was targeting Emma...to silence her."

Nate's stomach dipped. He swallowed, getting control of his emotions. On one hand, he was pissed. Emma's bleeding heart, as the General put it, had put her squarely on the radar of an international terrorist organization. Knowing her now, he was having a difficult time reconciling the journalist he'd been railing about for months with the warm, sweet, kind woman who'd shared his bed. If E.J. Lewis had just been some man with utopian ideals, he could've easily told him off for irresponsible journalism, the danger of so publicly supporting policies that encouraged asylum seekers while angering their oppressors and called it a day. But that wasn't the case. It was Emma. Kind-hearted Emma. The sweet woman who gave him a second chance at a first impression, which was rare. The spitfire, self-described nerd with beautiful legs and perfect breasts and an endearing habit of biting her lip just so...

"Any word from Interpol? Have they found al-Waleed?" Nate asked.

The general rubbed his chin. "No, not yet. He's still at large."

"Which means Emma is still in danger."

The men all sat forward looking at General Davidson expectantly.

"Then we need to get her back to D.C., into protective custody," he said. "Captain, I assume you'll want to be the one assigned to guarding her until we capture al-Waleed?"

"You assume correctly, sir." Nate wasn't about to let her fall under anyone else's protection. He might be pissed, but he wanted answers, and he wanted al-Waleed.

"We all will," said Doc. Eastwood, Skyscraper, Hollywood, and Ghost all nodded their agreement.

"Then let's get her back stateside ASAP. No communication will be allowed between her and any family, friends, or co-workers until this is resolved. Understood?"

"Sir, yes, sir," Nate replied. His head was spinning. Emma was in danger. The mere thought left him cold. He didn't know if there could be a relationship between them now, knowing what she did for a living, but her life had almost come to a tragic end. He couldn't let that happen again.

# Chapter 10

Emma stared out the window from the backseat of the black sedan. Nate sat next to her as the driver, a State Department security specialist, drove through the streets of Washington, D.C. Outside, a light rain was falling making the roads just slick enough to be dangerous in the near-freezing winter temperature. After being rescued from a kidnapping attempt by an international terrorist, Emma thought she'd be happy to be home. But that was not the case. Since her return to London, things hadn't gone at all as she'd hoped.

First of all, her vacation weekend was cut short. Second, she wasn't even allowed to see her friends, of whom she was sure were worried sick about her. When she'd arrived back at a British military base, she'd been whisked off to the American Embassy to be interviewed for hours. Three men in civilian suits, and one in an impressive British Navy uniform sat opposite her across a cold stainless-steel table inside a sterile white room. She'd sat there, shivering until someone gave her a blanket to wrap around her body. Emma was ready to burn the pink silk dress. She desperately wanted a bath, a change of clothes, and her bed. But everyone had insisted she be debriefed right away. She stared at her inquisitors, weary to the bone.

They introduced themselves as Agents Nelson and Leeks from MI6, Agent Jerry Marshall, CIA, and Commodore Brandon Andrews. They'd asked her the same questions over and over varying their order until they were satisfied she'd not somehow orchestrated her own kidnapping. The fact that it felt like they were even implying such a ludicrous scheme, after what she'd gone through, made her feel sick. Emma had already been terrified beyond belief, but to have these men stare her down like she was some kind of criminal broke something inside her. They were supposed to be the good guys. She was a good citizen, not some extremist journalist with an agenda. Yet they'd made her feel as if she needed to defend herself and every word she'd ever written. All she wanted was to leave that room, fall in Nate's arms and have him hold her.

She'd felt safe there when he rescued her. She wanted to feel safe again. But that didn't happen. Instead, she'd been told she couldn't contact her friends, her family, anyone she knew until al-Waleed was captured. Worse, she'd been told that her kidnapping wasn't a random event, but rather, she'd been targeted specifically for her recent articles in support of immigration reform for refugees seeking asylum. When she'd pointed out that her editor, Derek Riley, could also be in danger since he approved all her work for publication, the agents and the Commodore exchanged looks before Agent Marshall replied, "We'll take that into consideration."

That's all she got. Afterwards, she was taken to a military transport airplane where Nate was waiting. Relieved, she'd thrown herself into his arms, hugging his neck, but when he didn't return her embrace, Emma felt the bottom drop out of her world. All he'd said was that Becky and the girls would bring back her things from the hotel and that he and his men would be her personal security team until the threat against her was neutralized. She asked what was wrong, why all of this was happening and more importantly, why he was being so cold, but Nate clammed up, refusing to answer.

The only ones who offered her any kindness or sympathy were Allen and Doc. The rest of the men had gone into soldier mode.

It was a long and lonely flight home.

Now, as the sedan pulled up to a safehouse in a neighborhood not far from her own apartment, Emma unbuckled her belt, preparing to exit the vehicle as soon as it stopped. She didn't want to be this close to Nate anymore. She needed room, needed air.

"Wait!" Nate reached out to stop her from opening the door.

His hand grabbing hers was the first physical contact he initiated since the rescue. The tingles were still there, still strong as soon as his fingers circled her wrist, but the hurt and anger inside her was stronger.

Emma yanked her hand away. "Wait for what?"

Nate's eyes narrowed at the sharp edge in her tone. "Wait until I tell you it's okay to exit the car."

Emma huffed, pushing her glasses back up onto her nose. "So that's how it's going to be? You give orders and I meekly follow them?"

He watched her sitting there, openly defiant. She looked so small huddled within the leather jacket Ghost had lent her. Even so, her shoulders were squared, spine straight as a steel rod and her big brown eyes bore into his from behind her dark-rimmed spectacles. It was annoying to have his command questioned no matter how sexy and adorable she looked. Nate was caught between his own rising anger and equally rising desire to kiss her.

He needed to establish control. He stuck with anger. "Yes! That's the way it's going to be, Emma, until al-Waleed is captured and you're no longer in danger."

His retort struck her like a slap across the face. "Fine!" Emma turned, facing forward and stared angrily off into the distance.

The rigidity of her posture told Nate it most definitely was not fine. Taking it down a notch, he said, "I'm sorry. I shouldn't have been so blunt. Look, it's not ideal, I know, but it's for your own good. He already tried once and if we hadn't been able to respond quickly, you might already be..." His words trailed off and he struggled over the sudden lump in his throat.

Emma heard the hitch in his voice and softened, finishing his sentence.

"Dead."

She looked at Nate who stared out the opposite window. His rugged profile was as handsome as ever, but something about the man had changed, and she didn't know what she'd done to make him suddenly dislike her so much.

"Nate?"

He didn't answer, but the tension in his shoulders eased somewhat at the sound of his name on her lips.

Emma reached out, touching his arm. He flinched, and she retracted her hand quickly. Fighting back the hurt his reaction inflicted, she asked, voice wobbling, "What did I do?"

The pain in her words struck at his heart. Nate turned, about to reply when Hollywood opened Emma's door.

"All clear, Captain."

"You can get out now," said Nate. He exited his side of the vehicle and came around, scanning the area even as he gripped her arm and moved her quickly inside.

Emma swallowed hard. Her life had been flipped upside down in a matter of two days. She couldn't even go home and now she was stuck inside a small house on the northern end of D.C. with a man who didn't like her. As birthdays went, this one really sucked.

❧❧❧❧❧ ❧❧❧❧❧

Nate let the men find their spots within the three-bedroom house. Skyscraper and Hollywood took the first bedroom. Doc and Eastwood grabbed the second, and Ghost took the couch. That left the third bedroom for Emma. She was surprised when

Nate joined her, dropping his duffel bag on the floor next to the king-size bed.

"What are you doing?" she asked.

Nate looked at her. "I'm settling in."

Emma was standing by the window on the opposite side of the bed staring at him wide-eyed from behind her glasses. She was still wearing the hot pink silk dress and the jacket lent to her by Ghost on the way back across the Atlantic to keep her warm. She was dirty, tired, and wanted to be alone.

Nate reached down, unzipped his bag, and pulled out a pair of gray sweatpants and a black t-shirt. "You can change into these. They'll be a bit big on you, but there's nothing I can do about that right now." He paused. "I'm sorry we didn't have time to get your things from the hotel, Emma. I'll get you a pair of socks from Hollywood. He has the smallest feet. Tomorrow, I'll have someone bring you some clothes and shoes." He handed her a pad and pen from the nightstand. "Just write down your sizes and what you think you'll need."

Nate turned, heading out of the room.

"Wait." Emma stared at the clothes laid out on the bed and then at his back. Nate turned, watching her. "You're not sleeping in here with me."

His eyes narrowed. "Oh, yes, I am. You're not leaving my sight, Emma, not until this is over."

Seeing his determination, she blurted, "This is absurd! You don't even like me!" The words tumbled out of her mouth before she could stop them.

Nate let go of the door handle and stalked toward her, jaw clenched.

Emma backed up a step, suddenly wary. The wall at her back stopped her. The wall of his chest in front of her left her no way out. She was trapped.

"Emma, let me be perfectly clear. How I feel and what I think about someone does not matter. My job is to protect you until the threat on your life is resolved. To do my job, I need to keep you close and if that means sleeping in this bed with you then that's how it's going to be. So get used to the idea," he said, his voice dropping low, finger pointing at the large bed, "because both of us are sharing this bed together tonight and for however many nights it takes until this is over. Understand?"

Emma's heart raced, but she wasn't sure if it was anger at being given no choice in the matter or his nearness. She was still wildly attracted to him despite the fact she was mad as hell and hurt by his rejection. Worse, all her lady parts were jumping up and down in excitement, betraying her completely. *Bitches!*

"You can sleep on the floor then!"

Nate watched the sparks flashing in her eyes even as heat rose in her cheeks. She was breathing as if she'd run a marathon, causing her breasts to rise and fall in an appealing manner as she stubbornly stood her ground. In that moment, he forgot his anger and smiled wickedly, remembering she wasn't wearing much beneath that dress. Moving closer until barely an inch separated their bodies, he reached out touching the side of her face before sliding his finger down to her neck where he gently caressed the pulse point at her throat. "You can protest all you want," he whispered low, leaning in and grazing her jawline with his stubbled chin until his lips hovered over her ear. "But your body is sending out a very sweet invitation, Emma. I'd be happy to RSVP," he murmured, "personally."

Emma gasped when his lips caught the lobe of her ear, sucking it before dropping soft, hot kisses there and then working his way down the nape of her neck.

Her body responded, growing hot and needy. Nate nuzzled her, his hands sliding the jacket from her shoulders. Next, his thumbs hooked the straps of her dress, inching them down until her breasts were exposed to his view.

Sucking in a sharp breath, his hungry gaze took in every inch of her nakedness.

Emma couldn't even breathe. Her nipples were painfully hard, begging for his touch, but she was angry and hurt. Nate had run hot and cold since her rescue in France, and she still didn't know what she'd done besides getting kidnapped to cause it. Now she was stuck in a room with him and if he thought that meant he could just have his way with her to pass the time, he could just think again!

Taking a deep breath, she pulled the straps back up and pushed with all her strength past him. "I'm going to take a shower." Emma grabbed the clothes off the bed and marched into the bathroom, shoulders back and chin held high. When she slammed the door shut, he chuckled.

"What are you smiling about?" Ghost watched Nate enter the living room noting his captain grinning.

"Emma's mad at me."

"And that's funny?" Ghost raised a pale eyebrow.

"Not really, no."

Crossing his arms, Ghost glanced at Doc who sighed.

"I don't want to get in your business, Outlaw—"

"Then don't, Doc!" Nate snapped.

Ignoring his captain's outburst, Doc continued, "but she's been through a lot in the past two days. Maybe try and ease up on her. I don't know what's gotten into you, but two days ago, you really liked this little lady."

"She's the journalist he doesn't like," said Ghost.

"I know that. I was in that debriefing, but what's that got to do with anything? You know who she is now, not just some words on paper, not just some journalist with ideas different than your own, but a flesh and blood woman. So what if she's a bit of a bleeding heart. She cares about people. Nothing wrong with that even if your grumpy ass doesn't agree with it." Doc stated, pissing Nate off.

"He's just trying to find an excuse, Doc," said Ghost.

"An excuse for what?" asked Eastwood, entering the living room.

"To not care about Emma," Ghost replied.

"You mean no more than he already does?" Skyscraper threw in his two cents as he and Hollywood joined them.

"Too late, boss. You're already there. Otherwise, why would you insist on being her personal bodyguard? The State Department could've handled this, and you know it," Hollywood added.

Nate glared at his men. "Are you clowns finished?"

The men quieted. The look on their captain's face was one they knew well. It screamed, '*don't push your luck!*'

Nate stood with hands on hips. "Ghost, make a schedule. I want one man watching her apartment on eight-hour rotations. One of us stays here with her at all times. She doesn't leave this house. Get that written up and send out copies to the General, the State Department, and one to me. Understood?"

"Understood," said Ghost.

Nate nodded once and walked to the kitchen leaving the men alone.

"Man, he's got it bad," Hollywood chuckled.

"Yeah, but he's going to screw it up. Just watch," said Doc.

"Unless we help him," replied Ghost, lips twitching as he fought a grin.

# Chapter 11

Emma felt better after a hot shower, but it did nothing to cool her desire. Nate's kisses and raw male appeal had stoked a fire within and no amount of water pouring over her body could put it out. It got worse when she slipped into the clothes he lent her. The t-shirt smelled like his cologne from being packed in his duffel bag. She was surrounded by his scent, which annoyed her, but was also oddly comforting. After towel-drying her hair and pinning it up, she left the bathroom and found a pair of black socks folded on the end of the bed. She slid them on. Nate was right. Hollywood did have smallish feet because there wasn't much excess room. There was a joke in there somewhere and it would've been funny any other time, but not now. She didn't even have her friends to share it with.

Her stomach grumbled reminding her she hadn't eaten anything for the last twenty-four hours. She was hungry and tired, but before she could climb into bed and hopefully forget this nightmare for a while, she needed food.

Ghost was in the kitchen with Doc making spaghetti.

"Hungry, Emma?" Doc asked.

"Starving! That smells so good. Can I help you with anything?"

"No. We got it," said Ghost.

"Here, try this." Doc held out a stuffed mushroom from the tray he'd pulled out of the oven.

Emma took a bite of the appetizer. "This is so good. How'd you learn to cook like this?"

"My mom's a chef." Doc grinned, popping one of the mushrooms into his mouth.

"No kidding?" Emma smiled. "You know, Becky loves mushrooms."

"Oh, she does, does she?" Doc moved to stand by her. "And what else does freckles like?"

"Freckles?" Emma laughed.

"Yeah, well," Doc chuckled. "Give a guy the inside scoop, won't ya?"

"I will if you will," she sighed.

Doc and Ghost exchanged a look.

"What do you mean, Emma?" he asked.

She fidgeted, uncomfortable now having brought the subject up.

"Is everything okay with you and the captain?" Ghost inquired, dropping the spaghetti noodles into the pot of boiling water.

"I don't think it is," she said, staring at the floor tile.

Doc reached out, putting his arm around her shoulders. "He's just stressed. This whole situation has him on edge."

"You mean I have him on edge, getting myself kidnapped, and now he has to babysit me."

"That's not it at all, and it wasn't your fault. You did nothing wrong. What I meant was that Nate doesn't take on any mission he doesn't feel he can't handle," Doc explained.

She looked at him. "What do you mean he took this on? He's a soldier. I'm an assignment."

Ghost put the spoon down and faced her. "You've got that all wrong, Emma. Nate insisted on being the one to watch out for you. We all did," he said, looking at Doc who nodded his agreement.

"That's right. Old Nate wasn't about to let anything happen to his girl again, not after—"

"Not after your kidnapping," Ghost said, cutting Doc off.

"Yeah, right," said Doc, throwing a look of apology over her head at Ghost.

Emma digested his words, strange as they were. She looked up at Doc. "Did you just say 'his girl'?"

"Well, yeah," Doc grinned. "We haven't seen Nate so smitten in..." he thought for a moment, "a long time. He's damned protective of you, which kinda makes you one of us, sis." He squeezed her shoulders.

Emma bit her lip. She looked at Ghost who stood watching her. "Thank you, Allen." She returned Doc's hug. "Thanks, Doc."

"You're welcome, sis," he said.

Ghost stirred the noodles, tested one, and reached for the colander. "So, you about ready for some spaghetti?"

"I am, yes," she grinned.

"I'll go ring the dinner bell," said Doc, who poked his head out of the kitchen and yelled, "Dinner!"

Despite Doc's and Ghost's encouraging words, dinner was still awkward. Nate returned just as Skyscraper left to relieve Eastwood of watch over at her apartment. Emma had set aside a plate for Eastwood in the microwave for when he returned, and then filled one for herself. She entered the dining room and sat down next to Hollywood but as soon as Nate came in, Hollywood got up and moved to the other side of the table leaving the seat next to Emma vacant.

With Doc at one end and Ghost at the other, and Hollywood on one side holding the seat next to him for Eastwood, there was nowhere else for Nate to sit except at Emma's side. While he didn't have a problem with that, she did. As hungry as she'd been when she filled her plate, that feeling waned rapidly when Nate sat down, and she pushed her food around with her fork.

"Something wrong with the vittles, Emma?" Doc asked, a wicked twinkle in his green eyes.

Nate threw her a sideways glance as he downed a stuffed mushroom.

"No, no. Nothing. It's delicious," she said, twisting the noodles onto the fork and taking a bite.

"Good girl," said Doc. "Can't have you losing your curves. They're kinda nice. Aren't they nice, Outlaw?"

Emma blushed, staring at Doc in mortification. Her glasses slid down her nose and she automatically pushed them back up, clearing her throat.

Nate chewed slowly, giving Doc his poker face before turning to look at Emma. His eyes were drawn to the sight of her wearing his clothes. They were too big on her, but he still knew where every one of her curves were beneath the cotton. With her dark-rimmed glasses framing her big, brown eyes, her hair piled atop her head, and the pink tinge in her cheeks, she looked sexy as hell. She was studiously avoiding making eye contact and that annoyed him.

"They are, Doc," he said. His voice dropped low. "Very, very nice."

The heat in his tone made Emma gasp. Against her will, her eyes found his and the sizzle she expected wasn't there. Instead, his blue eyes were stormy with anger. Again, Emma didn't know what she'd done to earn his ire. She looked away quickly focusing on her food. Each bite was torture as Nate sat beside her watching her eat.

Finally, Ghost broke the silence. "How did the meeting go?" he asked.

Nate turned. "As expected. Nothing new yet. He slipped the French."

"Fucking French," Hollywood smirked. "It's no wonder we have to save their asses all the time."

"Be that as it may, we still have to find al-Waleed. I checked in with Rio and he says all's gone quiet in the back channels as of this morning. You know what that means." Nate looked around the table at the men.

"Yep," said Doc.

"Damn," Hollywood murmured.

Emma waited, but no explanation came. Curiosity got the better of her. "Well? What does it mean?"

Nate ignored her, working on clearing his plate.

Ghost answered. "It means he's on the move. When they go quiet, something's up and when something's up, they're making big plans or moving players around the board, so to speak."

"So there's no way to know who or where, right?" Emma asked.

"That's right," said Nate. "Not until their communication lines open up again or we get a confirmed sighting. Which means you don't leave my side," he added, throwing a pointed look in her direction.

Emma's eyes narrowed at the reminder. She opened her mouth to reply when Ghost cut her off.

"It's for the best, Emma. We're all here to keep you safe and we can't do that unless you cooperate. Anything less than your full compliance to Nate's rules right now puts us all in danger, and I know you don't want that."

She looked at Ghost, and then around the table at the men one by one. They waited patiently for her to understand the gravity of the situation.

For her part, Emma had come to know each of these men over the past forty-eight hours in a way that felt like she'd known them forever. They were funny, smart, kind, and brave. They were putting their lives on the line for her. The least she could do was her part in keeping them safe. Emma swallowed the lump in her throat.

"You're right, Allen." She fidgeted with her napkin and then looked at Nate who sat quietly watching her. "I'm sorry for being difficult. There's no excuse for that. You saved my life. I know you didn't have to. I'm sure you could've left it up to police or the French government to rescue me, but you didn't. You came for me." Her last words wobbled as her eyes welled with tears.

One slid down her cheek. Before he could stop himself, Nate reached out and wiped it away.

"How could I not?" The question was spoken softly, but what he said next shocked her. "I'll always come for you, Emma."

The silence around the table grew thick. Doc cleared his throat and pushed back his chair. "Anyone want seconds?"

Hollywood dabbed his eyes with his napkin. "None for me. You use too much garlic, Ghost. That shit has my eyes watering."

Ghost chuckled. "That's onions, Hollywood. Not garlic, you big wussy."

Nate rested his hand on top of Emma's, threading his fingers with hers. Watching his men dissemble into a bunch of emotional women was awkward at best, but it wasn't nearly as awkward as his own surprising words to Emma. He wasn't sure where that had come from, but he meant what he'd said. He would always come for her, and having arrived at that conclusion, something shifted in his heart. His anger dissolved. It was never her fault, just his own stubbornness over an issue that wasn't even important. She was who she was, and he liked her. He felt lighter than he had for a long time, as if a weight had been lifted from his shoulders. And it was all because of Emma.

Emma bit her lip. She was grateful for the break in the silence. She could breathe again. Nate's thumb caressed the back of her hand absently. While the men refilled their plates and poked fun at each other, she and Nate gazed into each other's eyes, a new understanding between them blossoming with each passing moment.

Nate looked at Emma's near-empty plate. "Are you finished?"

She glanced at the last few bites remaining and nodded. "Yes."

"Good." Nate pushed back his chair and stood. Still holding her hand, he said, "there's something I want to tell you." He waited as she rose, standing beside him. Swallowing hard, he took a deep breath, leading the way out of the dining room to the bedroom. He needed privacy for this conversation, one he'd shared with only one other individual. But now that he'd found Emma, it was time.

# Chapter 12

E mma's heart ached. The story Nate shared made her ache for the man, but it also explained so much.

"It wasn't your fault, Nate," she said, holding his hand as they sat opposite each other on the end of the bed.

"It was, Emma. I was supposed to be there." He dropped her hand and got up, pacing. "It was our engagement party, dammit. A family event. Our daughter, Charlie, was with us. She was only a year old," he said, pulling his wallet out of his back pocket. There, tucked safely inside one of the leather folds was a picture of a blue-eyed baby girl with dark gold curls. The last picture taken of Nate's daughter. He looked at it as he had hundreds of times since that night. With care, he showed Emma. "Jessica and I named her Charlotte after her grandmother and Marie after mine. I called her Charlie," he smiled. "But then my pager went off and I had to leave. You know, we can't just ignore it. As a Green Beret, I'm on call 24/7 and I can't stop and offer explanations. What we do is top secret."

"I understand," said Emma.

"Do you?" Nate's voice was tortured. "Because I don't think Jessica ever really did. How could she? It took a year after Charlie's birth just to have enough time to get engaged, to plan the party. I had to leave before we even cut the cake. She said she would call a cab and be okay, but that's not what happened. Instead, she decided to walk the ten blocks home. I don't know why the hell she did that! And with Charlie." Anger poured out of him as his hands flexed. "The last we knew of her whereabouts was a security camera two blocks from our apartment in Fort Carson. She stopped in to the convenience store on the corner and when she came out, a man followed her. He'd been standing outside near the gas pumps. That's how he was caught. Got his face clear as day on video. He was an illegal from Mexico. Been deported twice and was still back in the country. He had a rap sheet a mile long. Robbery, possession, assault, known links to MS13. Jessica tried to defend herself. I don't even know how she survived, but Charlie..." his voice trailed off.

Emma went to him, wrapping her arms around his waist and pressing her face into his chest. "I'm so sorry, Nate."

His arms went around her automatically, seeking the comfort he'd denied himself for so long. Nate leaned into her hair, inhaling the floral scent. "It wasn't the same afterwards. She couldn't forgive me. I couldn't forgive myself. In the end, she left, moving back to Texas."

Emma didn't know what else to say. Nate had lost everything doing his duty. It wasn't fair. His job was to protect people and yet because of that job, he felt he'd failed to protect the two most important people in his life. She felt his pain keenly and wanted only to take it away.

"I'm sure Jessica doesn't blame you, Nate. Did she ever say that she did?" she looked up at him.

His blue eyes were haunted with old ghosts. "Not in so many words."

"There. See? She never said it. She was hurting too. That's all. Nate," she said, reaching up, touching his face, "forgive yourself."

"I can't," he whispered. "Charlie..."

"She would want you to forgive yourself too."

"How do you know that?" he said, raw with emotion.

"Because, she was your daughter. And if the situation was reversed somehow, you wouldn't want her blaming herself, being so unhappy. It's what you would tell her...so follow your own advice. It will bring you both peace."

Nate knew she was right but letting go after holding on to the pain for so long wasn't easy. It was part of him, and he felt like letting it go would be like losing Charlie all over again.

"I don't know if I can, Emma."

She held his head, caressing his hair. "You can, Nate. She'll always be with you," she said, reaching out a hand to touch his chest, "right here, safe in your heart, forever."

Nate leaned into her hand and lowered his forehead until it touched hers. Slowly, their breathing synced as they stood holding each other.

"I'm sorry." His softly spoken words felt like a balm on Emma's heart.

"Me too."

"What are you sorry about?" His eyes searched hers.

"Whatever it is I did to make you not want to be around me anymore." She swallowed, her gaze falling away and fixating on his shirt.

Nate groaned, pulling her closer. "Emma, you didn't do a thing. It's all on me. I've been an ass and you didn't deserve it. Any of it."

"But you've been avoiding me since we got back to London. I know I messed up leaving your room and going off in a strange place on my own, and then when you said it's because I made myself a target with the articles I've written..."

Nate placed a finger over her lips. "Stop. Look at me." He slid the finger under her chin tilting her face up to his. "It was me. When I found out you were E.J. Lewis, the same writer whose articles I'd been reading, it threw me, okay? I've had to reconcile the journalist to the woman I got to know. And you didn't do anything wrong. Terrorists are sick assholes who fixate on crazy shit. You can't go around walking on eggshells trying not to set one off. You'd be crazy. Also, your articles, while perhaps naïve where terrorists are concerned, are well-written and intelligent. Maybe a little too 'pie in the sky' sometimes for my tastes, but then, I'm jaded. Hard not to be doing what I do, but you have heart, Emma. I know that now. You care about people. It's a special quality. You're a special woman. You don't have a damn thing to apologize for."

Emma was floored. Her mouth had fallen open somewhere around his admission that he read her articles and despite not liking hearing she was naïve about anything, he'd said she was a good writer, intelligent, and...special.

Nate noticed her shocked expression and lack of response to his words. "What?"

"You read my articles," she said, smiling, and then leaned up on tip-toes kissing him.

Stunned for a moment, Nate kissed her back. It began in sweet exploration but quickly escalated into blazing passion.

He pulled away, panting. "Are you sure?" he asked.

"Oh yes. I'm sure," she grinned.

"Thank God," he growled.

In no time, he'd stripped her naked and laid her upon the bed where he proceeded to show her just how special she'd become to him in such a short time. This time, it wasn't just a joining of bodies. It was a joining of hearts.

In the wee hours of the morning, they lay entwined, skin against skin, sated.

"Nate?" she whispered.

"Mm-hmm?" he murmured, eyes closed, his arms holding her close.

"You really read my articles?"

He chuckled. "Yes, Emma. I really do."

"But you think I'm naïve..." she shifted away and he pulled her back to him.

"I didn't mean it like that. It was more about not knowing the uglier side of what you write about where terrorists are concerned. Honestly, honey, that's a good thing. But now," he paused, raising a hand to tuck a stray strand behind her ear, "now you've seen some of it. You've been in a terrifying situation. I wish I could turn back the clock and prevent that from ever happening."

"But you can't," she said. Snuggling closer, she added, "still, the fact that you wish you could means everything to me. One good thing, at least..." she teased.

Nate waited, and when she didn't answer, he asked, "What?"

"Any future articles I write won't have that same naivete anymore. That should help keep your blood pressure down."

"There's always that," Nate agreed.

Emma gasped, slapping his shoulder. "Nate!"

He laughed, grabbing her hand and carrying it to his lips. He dropped light kisses on her fingers. "I was only kidding. Truth is, I'll miss that." He rolled, pulling her atop his body. "I kind-of liked naïve Emma." He gazed at her face taking in her tumbled hair and kiss-swollen lips. "She's a treasure. A woman of heart and fiery passion."

Smiling, Emma squirmed atop him, wrapping her legs around his waist as she drew a line over the stubble on his cheek. "So you don't like me now?"

Nate groaned, grinning at the wanton woman growing bolder and more confident with every passing minute. He glanced down at her breasts pressed against his chest and with wicked intent, rolled his hips, thrusting his rising desire into her sensitive core. She sucked in a sharp breath, biting her lip.

"I like you more than I should," he whispered, watching the sexy expression on her sweet face as he rolled his hips again. "Maybe I need to show you again because I think you forgot about earlier already and repetition, as I'm sure you know, helps memory, Miss Lewis."

Nate quickly reversed their positions and in one smooth motion, slid deep inside her warmth.

"Oh my gosh, yes," she groaned. "Show me."

"Hang on, baby." Nate swiveled and then thrust deep, increasing the pace, all the while watching Emma lose herself in the pleasure.

They made love, each giving, each taking, until the world exploded in a million pieces. As they lay catching their breath, Nate leaned up on his elbow staring into Emma's eyes. He smiled slowly.

"What? she asked. "What are you smiling about?"

He shook his head and touched her hair, winding a strand around his finger. "When this is over, I want to take you out on a proper date. Anywhere you want."

Emma grinned. "Oh yeah?"

"Yeah," he answered softly.

"Okay. It's a date."

Nate gathered her close, settling them both in as he pulled the covers up around her shoulders. Content and exhausted, they finally slept.

When Emma woke the next morning, Nate was gone.

# Chapter 13

E ven though she was disappointed to find him already up and out the door, Emma was happy. The world was a rosier place, except for the fact that a brutal terrorist was after her. But besides that, she couldn't stop smiling. Nate was the reason. His touch thrilled her. His kisses melted her bones and the things he did to her body should probably be illegal, but it was the way he made her feel that was the cherry on top of her sundae. He liked her. A lot, he'd said, and he'd shown her several times over. Not just in bed, but with his actions. He'd risked his life to save hers. He was, even now, putting himself between her and a killer. And then when she'd stepped out of the shower, there were packages of new clothes sitting on the bed.

Hollywood said they been delivered by a State Department flunkie, but that Nate had ordered the items himself.

For Emma, it was like receiving a bunch of birthday presents from her boyfriend.

*Her boyfriend.*

She liked the way that sounded in her head. She loved that he was so thoughtful in picking out clothing for her. There were three pairs of jeans, four sweaters in colors that complemented her hair and eyes, a pair of athletic shoes and one pair of dark brown leather hiking boots. In another bag was socks and hair products, and a makeup kit for brunettes, but it was the last bag that sent a flush to her cheeks. It was filled with the laciest, prettiest matching sets of bras and panties. Emma didn't own such finery. She usually wore cotton bikinis and sports bras and was lucky if the colors matched. Even so, they were all so pretty and all of this must've cost a fortune. At the bottom of the lingerie bag was a small box wrapped in light blue paper tied with silky white ribbon. A card attached read, "Happy birthday, Emma. Yours, Nate."

*Her Nate.* Grinning like an idiot, she held the card to her heart.

She tore into the box, unable to quell her excitement. Inside was a heart-shaped locket in white gold. It was engraved with intricate filigree and hung on a delicate chain. She couldn't suppress the smile that bloomed on her face if she'd tried.

After choosing a red, sweetheart neckline sweater and a pair of jeans, she slid on the brown leather boots. How he knew she'd prefer hiking boots over the fashionable variety, she didn't know, but it pleased her. Everything fit perfectly. Looking in the mirror, she put the necklace on and admired the completed ensemble. She was dressed head to toe in gifts from Nate. Her skin glowed with happiness and a giggle burst from her lips. She was looking forward to later. She was sure he'd picked out the lacy lingerie more as a gift to himself, and that thought caused warmth to spread throughout her body and settle low.

With one last glance in the mirror, she left the bedroom and found Eastwood and Skyscraper in the living room playing cards.

They looked up when she walked in.

"Good morning, Emma," Eastwood said, noticing her outfit. "I see you got your goodies."

"I did," she grinned. "How do I look?" She struck a pose.

Skyscraper chuckled. "Girl, you know you look good."

"Well, I had a little help. Can't believe Nate knows so much about women's clothes. And he picked out my kind of footwear." She looked down at her boots.

"Yeah, but I'm sure he was thinking more about undressing you," Eastwood smirked, tossing a card down onto the table. "One, dealer."

"Why you gotta be so crass, man?" said Skyscraper, dealing out a card and sliding it across the table. "Ignore him, Emma. He doesn't get to be around ladies often and doesn't know how to act."

"Aw, I didn't mean anything. Emma knows that. Look at her," he said, glancing her way. "She's a smitten kitten, aren't ya?"

Emma laughed. "I think Marcus is right. Maybe we can work on your social graces later. Who's up for a short walk?"

The guys looked at her. "In the middle of the game? I'm up by ten dollars here. Plus, until Nate gets back, we need to stay inside. We haven't reconned the neighborhood yet this morning. Until we know it's safe, no going out for you."

Emma's mood sank. She looked out the window, sighing. "Okay."

The men resumed their game, oblivious of her presence. Emma went to the kitchen for coffee and breakfast. As she stared out the window above the sink, a low 'mew' interrupted her thoughts. She leaned over the sink, scanning the side yard. On the ledge outside was a tiny orange kitten.

"Oh, my goodness, where'd you come from?"

*"Mew. Mew,"* it answered, pawing the window.

"Oh, sweet baby." She walked to the sliding glass door and paused. She knew she shouldn't go out alone. Emma leaned back and looked into the living room. The guys were dealing out a new hand and she didn't want to disturb them. It was just the side yard. No reason why she couldn't take five steps out, pick up the kitten, and be right back before they even knew it. She slid the door open and poked her head out. Looking left and right to make sure the coast was clear, she dashed out to get the kitty.

⁂

Nate was in a foul mood. His meeting with the general and State Department officials had not gone well. He'd made an assumption based on very little information and he'd been wrong.

"We identified all the deceased in the pictures your team provided from the mission in Prague," said the woman to his left.

Natalie Greenblatt was an ex-Marine intelligence officer now working for the SD. Her specialty was identifying and cataloging terrorists. Her work helped thwart many terrorist attacks before they had a chance to get off the ground.

The general glared at her. "Get on with it, Natalie."

She pursed her lips, but continued, looking at Nate. "One of the men you killed was Tariq al-Waleed," Nate tensed, waiting for her to finish, "Mohammed al-Waleed's younger brother."

He sat back in his chair regarding the three people in the room. Next to Natalie was the aid to the Secretary of State, Adam Jones, an aspiring prick with a stick up his ass. Nate could smell the ambition rolling off him in nauseating waves. He and Jones had butted heads several times before. *Why would today be any different*, he thought.

"So?"

"Goddammit, Captain!" the general bellowed. "Don't you get it yet? Waleed isn't after the journalist, he's after you! She's just in the way and as far as he's concerned, an expendable knife to drive into your gut. Now how the hell did this bastard manage to track you to London, that's what I want to know because you assured me you were not followed?"

Jones smirked, watching Nate. "Yes, Captain, just what protocol did you break to lead a terrorist to a private American citizen?"

Nate bit his tongue. More than anything, he wanted to reach across the table and punch Jones in his smug face, but he couldn't. In the presence of General Davidson, he had to control himself. Plus, there was a lady present. As he pondered just how al-Waleed could've possibly tracked them, Natalie's cell phone rang. She glanced at the screen, prepared to hit IGNORE, but the number displayed stopped her.

"Sorry, sir," she looked at the general, "but I should answer this." She got up and walked to the corner. "Greenblatt here. What've you got?"

The general grunted. "Someone's head's gonna roll for this one, Captain. I'm not taking this beating alone. We have a goddamn terrorist hunting an American citizen, damned near had her, all because someone blew your cover. We were able to keep it quiet, but he's not finished, and I guaran-damn-tee you when he strikes again, I will be kicking ass and taking names!"

"General, you need to hear this,' Natalie interrupted. She put her phone on speaker, setting it down on the table. "Go ahead. We can all hear you now."

"General Davidson, I bet you're fit to be tied but I have some news that will make it a bit better."

Recognizing the voice, the general barked, "Rio, you sonofabitch. You damn-well better have found that scumbag because that's the only thing that's going to make this right."

"Nate? You there?" Rio asked.

"I'm here, buddy."

"Good, because it wasn't your fault. You didn't fuck up."

"Say again?" the General demanded.

"It wasn't Nate or his men. There's a mole, sir. A traitorous little fuck who happened to know about the snatch-and-grab in Prague. His name is Jamal Almasi and he's an asset for the French government. Someone in their own camp allowed Almasi too much access to information. He's their contact within Black Jihad. I'd say either al-Waleed found out Almasi's a double agent or the little shit has been playing both sides against the middle the entire time. Either way, it wasn't Nate or his team. They were given up by insider French intelligence—"

"Incompetent sonsofbitches!" the General exploded. "Goddammit."

Jones, seeing the meeting going sideways from his own agenda spoke. "That really doesn't excuse Captain Oliver—"

"Shut the hell up, Adam!" The General addressed Rio next. "Tell me you got a fix on al-Waleed, Rio."

"I don't, sir." Rio paused. They could hear typing in the background. "But I have a fix on Almasi, and he's not in Qatar or France. He's in Washington D.C."

Nate jumped out of his chair. "The fuck you say!" He leaned over the phone placing his hands on the table. "Where, Rio? Where is he right now?"

Rio rattled off an address. "That cell phone he uses to communicate with his handler in the French government has been pinging steadily there for the last hour."

General Davidson looked at Nate who glanced at Natalie.

"That's the safehouse. My men are there. Emma is there. How the hell did you miss him coming into the country, Natalie?" Nate's voice grew in volume with his anger.

"Call your men and get your ass back there now. We can't let him get away this time, Captain." The General stood, clearly rattled. He turned stern eyes on Natalie and Adam Jones. "And you two better damn-well figure out how you fucked up. You have one job. Keep the goddamn terrorists out! Homeland Security should've been alerted immediately. And this better be kept in house. If I see even one story hit the news, heads will roll!"

"Yessir," Natalie replied. She left the room.

Jones got up grabbing the file folder he'd carried in from the table. "The Secretary is going to want a full briefing."

"And I'm sure you'll spoon-feed it to him and then wipe his ass later, but for now, you keep this on the down-low, Adam. If this spins out into the public, it'll cause a panic. People will get hurt, innocent civilians, and it will be on your head. I'll make goddamn sure of it!" The General pointed a finger in Jones' face punctuating his remarks.

Nate watched the exchange, his cell phone already in hand. General Davidson turned angry eyes to Nate. "Well? What are you waiting for? Dismissed!"

"Sir. Yes, sir!" Nate saluted the general, and then he ran out of the room, hitting speed-dial as he made his way quickly to the SUV issued to him on loan from the State Department.

The phone rang twice before Eastwood picked up.

"What's up, Captain?"

"Eastwood, al-Waleed's got someone watching the house. He's there now. Rio confirmed it."

Shock echoed in Eastwood's voice. "That motherfu—"

"Where's Emma?" asked Nate, frantic. He got into the SUV and cranked the ignition, pulling out of the parking lot.

"She's in the kitchen. Hold on." There was a pause and then, "Shit!"

"What? Dammit, Eastwood, what?"

"She was here, Nate, I swear. Skyscraper and I were in the living room. She went into the kitchen to get coffee, but now she's gone. And the side door is open."

Nate felt the air leave his body. Eastwood's words were like a punch to the gut. "Find her! I'll be there in ten minutes. Canvas the neighborhood and call Doc and Hollywood. Tell them to get back there pronto. That's a damned order!"

# Chapter 14

"Show me the closed-circuit footage," Nate demanded as he strode into the house.

The safehouse was wired with inconspicuous security cameras all around the perimeter. Eastwood tapped the keys on the computer screen and pulled up each feed. In seconds, he found what they were looking for. On the east side of the house, the camera facing the sliding glass door to the kitchen showed that door opening. Emma leaned out, looking both ways before stepping out and turning left. She walked up to the kitchen windowsill where she scooped a small ball of fluffy fur into her hands. It was a kitten. Nate grunted, biting his tongue. *She'd gone outside for a kitten.* As she turned to come back in, a figure dressed in black from head to toe wearing a ski mask ran up behind her, one arm snaking around her waist while the other hand clamped over her mouth. She dropped the kitten who ran off, terrified.

The figure dragged her brutally to a gray van where he threw her inside the waiting vehicle. When Emma rallied, trying to push past him to safety, he punched her in the face, sending her reeling into the van's interior. He then slid the door shut, locked it from the outside, and quickly drove away heading north.

The team remained silent while their leader fumed. They knew how painful it was for him to see that happen to his lady. Eastwood and Skyscraper were particularly quiet.

Pacing, Nate ran a hand over his face. "Tap into the city's CCTV network and get me a fix on that van," he said.

"On it," Eastwood replied.

Without missing a beat, Nate speed-dialed Rio. "Rio, she was taken from the safe house."

"Shit. I'm sorry man. What do you need?"

"I need to know where he is. Tell me you're still tracking that cell phone."

The sound of keys tapping in the background filled the silence as Rio did what Rio does. "It's pinging off the north tower near the Union Market warehouse district. He's there. Closest I can figure is the southeast corner."

"Thanks, Rio. I knew I could count on you."

"Go get your girl, Outlaw." Rio hung up.

Nate addressed his team. "Saddle up, boys. We're not letting this fucker get away. Shoot to kill, but if any one of you puts Emma in danger, I'll throttle you myself."

"We'll get her, Captain," said Skyscraper. "And we're sorry. This is our failure," he said, standing next to Eastwood.

"Yeah. It's on us, man." Eastwood stood up next to Skyscraper, accepting full responsibility.

Nate glared at his men. He was angry as hell, but he'd seen the footage. Emma didn't obey orders. She thought she'd be safe stepping out to rescue a kitten. A kitten! And she should've been, too. No, the only person truly at fault here was him. He'd been the target, not Emma like he'd previously thought. Only because of him was she in danger at all. He'd put her in harm's way because he'd been drawn to her. Something about her had pulled him in, opened his heart. That was the amazing gift she'd given him and what had he done in return? Got her kidnapped. Twice!

He swallowed. Mea culpas didn't come easy for him, especially as team leader. "It's not your fault. I'm the one who brought her into this mess. Turns out the French asset, Jamal Almasi, tipped off al-Waleed as to our whereabouts. It's all about revenge because we killed that terrorist-fuck's little brother in Prague. He was the one guarding Penelope Rand. Right now, we don't know if Almasi betrayed our location in London willingly or not, but he's tracked us here and he has Emma. No doubt on Waleed's orders. That's his cell phone signal Rio tracked and right now, he's in a warehouse in Union Market. For how long, we don't know, so let's stop giving each other hand-jobs and let's get our asses on the move."

"Yes, sir!" They replied.

Within five minutes, they were loaded up in the SUV and on the road.

The old warehouse district was designated as historical by the city. Much of it was being revitalized, but the Depression-era buildings still maintained the appearance of bygone days. Several were occupied with meat processing plants, produce storage, and one was an old fish packing business. Doc drove the SUV to the southeast corner at Nate's direction. In the passenger seat, cradling his M4 Carbine assault rifle, Nate scanned the vehicles parked around the backs and sides of each building. When they reached the last one, they found what they were looking for. A gray van sat parked on the side of the old seafood warehouse near the back door.

"That's it. Pull around back, Doc," Nate said. "Eastwood, you and Sky take the back entry. Hollywood, you and Doc take the front. Ghost," he looked back over his shoulder. "You're with me at the side door. Everyone get in position and on my mark—storm the castle. We're going to send this cockroach running."

"Roger that," they replied.

In the busy district where trucks moved in and out, no one noticed six men exiting a dark, government-issued SUV dressed in camo and black. Each carried high-powered assault rifles, were strapped to the teeth with weapons, and protected by Kevlar. The men fanned out, moving quickly in pairs to their designated entry points.

Nate and Ghost stopped outside the side door.

"Check for wires," said Nate.

Ghost nodded. He inspected the hinges and slid a razor-thin card through the crease between the door and the jamb. "No wires there. Stand back." Ghost reached for the doorknob as Nate stepped back and to the side. Carefully, he turned the knob and cracked it open an inch, checking the visible areas. He glanced over his shoulder. "No explosives."

"Good." Nate clicked the communication device at his shoulder. "Everyone clear?" He knew the men would perform the same check on their entry points per training.

"All clear, Captain," said Hollywood.

"Clear here, Outlaw," Skyscraper replied.

"Then on my mark. Three, two, one!" Upon Nate's countdown, Ghost threw the door wide and entered low, ready to shoot. The side door led to a small office. There was no one inside.

"Clear," he announced.

Nate moved in hard on his heels, sweeping the room. "Through there," he pointed with the tip of his rifle at a second door. It was an interior office door with a glass panel. They could see into the hallway and entered carefully, each facing the opposite direction.

"Which way?" Ghost waited for the command.

Nate glanced left. He knew Hollywood and Doc could handle the front end. "Right."

They moved right with Nate taking the lead. Ghost protected his back.

A series of offices and closets lined this hallway. All were empty. Frustrated, Nate doubled back in the opposite direction. If Almasi was here, he was somewhere in the interior of the warehouse.

When they reached the other end of the hall, they found a door leading to the fish packing room. It was massive, filled with conveyor belts that had not been used for some time. The stench of rotten fish still lingered on the stale air as specs of dust danced in the dim light filtering in from windows placed high in the walls. Across the room a door opened.

Nate and Ghost took aim immediately but relaxed a notch when they saw Hollywood and Doc entering.

"Anything?" Nate asked.

"We didn't find a thing," said Doc.

Suddenly, the light turned on and the conveyor belts screeched into motion.

"What the fuck?" Ghost began sighting around the room looking for a target.

"He's here," said Nate. "Stay sharp, gentlemen." Each man moved closer to cover.

The large hooks hanging at the far end of the conveyor on an overhead rail began to move. The rail extended inside a massive freezer behind plastic sheeting. Something small and wriggling came through those plastic flaps. It was suspended on a hook heading for the large steel saw.

"Emma!" Nate jumped, running to her. "Ghost, cut the power!"

Ghost looked for the power switch while Doc followed Nate. Hollywood searched the room from his vantage point providing cover for Nate and Doc.

The hook from which Emma hung upside down by her ankles, inched closer to the large rusty saw.

"Emma, I'm here!" Nate jumped up onto the conveyor belt.

Emma, her face bruised a bright purple, bucked wildly. With her hands tied behind her back and tape over her mouth, she was helpless. Nate balanced on the conveyor belt between the saw and Emma. He had one chance to lift her shackled feet off the hook. Otherwise, she was headed straight for the spinning blade. He couldn't let that happen. He'd die first!

"Ghost!" he shouted, bracing himself.

"I can't find the switch," he hollered back, flipping every switch he could find.

"Cut the wires!" Nate screamed, arms out ready to grab Emma around the waist.

Frantic, Ghost stopped searching for the right switch in the massive warehouse and instead, located the tangle of power cords tied together against the far wall. He aimed his M4 at the knot of cords and pulled the trigger. The deafening sound of machine gun fire filled the space. Lights went off. Some machines ceased, but the saw continued to spin and the line of hooks advanced.

Nate reached out, wrapping his arms around Emma and lifted, but the continued motion of the conveyor belt thwarted his effort. Her feet didn't clear the hook. Nearly falling backwards,

Nate spun around, repositioning himself to the other side, now desperately trying to balance and lift at the same time. They were almost upon the deadly blade.

"Emma, when I count to three, kick as hard upwards as you can, okay?"

Emma nodded, fear filling her eyes.

"Good girl. One, two, three!" Nate lifted her body with all he had. Emma kicked up.

The ankle shackles cleared the tip of the hook and they fell onto the conveyor belt together, inches from the blade.

Nate rolled her over his body and threw her to the floor, his back now to the rusty saw. Ghost fired off another round and the warehouse went silent as the power shut down.

Panting, Nate looked behind him. The blade, now stilled, was one inch from his spine.

Sending up a silent prayer of thanks, he moved off the belt and dropped down to Emma's side, pulling the tape off her mouth before gathering her into his arms.

"Nate, oh my God! Oh my God!" The words tumbled from her lips in a stream as he held her.

"Sssh, I know. I'm so sorry, Emma. I'm here, baby. I'm here."

A slow clap interrupted their moment.

"Isn't that touching?" A man's voice cut through the silence.

Nate looked up. On the scaffolding above stood not Jamal Almasi, but Mohammed al-Waleed.

"You sonofabitch!" Nate stood, pulling Emma up beside him. He positioned himself in front of her. Waleed's presence answered one question for Nate. Jamal Almasi was dead. It was his phone they'd been tracking, the one issued to him by the French government. "You really are a coward, Waleed, going after children, kidnapping and beating women."

Al-Waleed didn't take the bait. "Not a coward, soldier boy, but a great warrior who knows how to strike where I will do the most damage."

"They're innocent! Penelope Rand is not a soldier. Emma isn't a soldier. Hell, for that matter, you're not one either. You're just a filthy fucking terrorist."

The man smiled but it did not reach his eyes. He glanced to Nate's right catching Ghost taking aim. "I wouldn't do that if I were you, haint." Waleed raised his hand, showing the device he was holding.

Ghost ignored the insult, keeping the terrorist in his crosshairs.

"You're not going to pull that trigger, Waleed. You're too much of a pussy to die with us." Nate caught sight of Hollywood and Doc out of the corner of his eye. Doc leaned out from behind a column, his hand pointing up at the far right of the scaffolding. Nate sent him a hand signal behind his back acknowledging the information.

"So vulgar. Just like all Americans. Low-down dogs undeserving to live. No, I won't be dying with you today. This is a remote detonator. Of course, if you shoot me and my fingers accidentally push the button, we'll all die, but I still won't lose.

I'll be meeting Allah while you all will burn in hell like the infidels you are."

"Allah would be disgusted by you. Read your fucking Quran, Waleed. Just like our Bible, it says 'thou shalt not kill.'"

"And what of your God? You kill. Or else why are you a soldier, soldier boy?" Something shifted in Waleed's eyes. "After all, you killed my brother!"

Nate knew he'd hit a nerve. "You mean that weak piece of shit holding a little girl hostage? Yeah, he went down fast. Bullets cut through Tariq like a hot knife through butter."

"Shut up! You are not worthy of speaking his name!" Al-Waleed's face twisted with rage.

"And what kind of big brother are you? Why was little brother even there? You want to blame me for his death, but who put him in harm's way? Who failed to protect him? You, Waleed. You are to blame for Tariq's death. So why don't you shove your detonator right up your ass?"

Waleed reached behind him, whipping out a Sig 9 mm tucked into his pants. He pointed it at Nate. "You will not die first, you dog! No, but you will suffer. You will watch your whore die." He aimed left over Nate's shoulder at Emma.

Shots fired. Nate threw Emma to the ground, covering her body with his own.

Waleed fell forward, flipping over the railing and landing hard on the concrete below with a loud crack.

Eastwood came running across the scaffolding, Skyscraper at his back.

Below, Hollywood and Ghost rushed to retrieve the detonator. The red light in the center began to flash. The timer had been triggered.

"Shit," Ghost sputtered. He looked up at the scaffolding. "Eastwood, we need you now!" he shouted at the man. The red-bearded soldier raced for the stairs.

Arriving on the floor, he ran to Ghost's side taking the detonator.

"Thirty seconds," he said, as he pulled out a pocketknife and began unscrewing the back of the device.

As he worked, Outlaw and Skyscraper searched the warehouse for explosives.

Outlaw shouted at Doc. "Get Emma out of here!"

Eastwood removed the back of the detonator carefully and pulled out the cluster of wires.

"Which one kills it?" Ghost asked.

Eastwood eyed the three wires. "The red one, usually. Or blue if no red."

Ghost stared hard at them. "They're all black!"

"I know!" said Eastwood, his brows knitted together. "Shut up while I think!"

"There's only maybe ten seconds left!"

"Dammit, Ghost!" Eastwood swore and then cut the first wire.

The red flashing light kept flashing.

"Fuck!"

"Cut them all!" Ghost ordered.

"I can't! One of these will set off the explosives!" Eastwood glared at Ghost.

"Well, do something!"

The red-bearded soldier blew a bead of sweat off his forehead and stared at the wires. "Eenie, meenie, miney, and....moe!" he shouted, then squeezed his eyes shut and cut the next wire.

Seconds ticked by. Eastwood cracked open one eye and looked at the detonator. The red light was no longer flashing, no longer lit.

Next to him, Ghost sighed.

"Holy shit," he muttered. "That was close."

"Found the C4," Skyscraper announced. The tall man stood near the southwest corner of the room. High up on a support column was the explosive compound stuck to the beam.

"Call in ordnance, Skyscraper. Can't leave that here," Outlaw ordered.

"Later days, fucker," said Eastwood, looking down on Waleed's dead and broken body. He tossed the now useless detonator down next to the dead terrorist.

Skyscraper glanced his way, his eyes falling on al-Waleed. "Cracked like a pinata. Score one for the good guys. Oh, and I ain't worried about going to hell, either. I only shoot bad guys."

"Amen, brother." Eastwood grinned.

Doc poked his head back inside the door. When Outlaw gave him the "all clear" signal, he brought Emma back in, staying near the exit, just in case.

"You okay, Emma?" Skyscraper asked.

Emma looked at the men, tears staining her cheeks. She offered a wobbly smile. "I'm here."

Eastwood stood and turned, looking at her. "We're sorry, Emma. We were supposed to be looking out for you."

Staring at the broken body of al-Waleed, Emma shuddered. That could very easily have been her...or one of the men. Could have been Nate. The thought made her nauseous. "It's not your fault, guys. I went outside. You told me not to, and I didn't listen. I thought I'd be okay just going to the window." Emma hiccoughed as fresh tears fell. "I'm so sorry."

Nate pulled her close, kissing her hair. "You have nothing to be sorry for, sweetheart. He came after you because of me. Because we killed his brother rescuing a little girl."

"What? You mean it wasn't because of my writing?" she asked through sobs.

"Nope. Guess your writing isn't that bad after all," Nate said. Then, "Sorry, bad joke."

"I'd hit you for that but my hands," she said through tears, pulling at the restraints.

"Oh, damn. Sorry, baby. Let's get that taken care of right now." Nate glanced at Doc. "This whole building is wired with explosives. We need to clear the warehouse district immediately."

"On it, Captain," said Doc, who then turned a dimpled smile to Emma. "Glad you're okay, Emma."

"Me too, Doc."

Nate reached down, scooping Emma up in his arms. "Let's get you out of here first and then we'll remove those shackles."

"Yes, please. Just get me home. I want to go home, Nate." All of the tension and anxiety over the last several hours left Emma drained. She was bone-weary and exhausted physically and emotionally. She'd seen too much, been through too much trauma, and all she wanted was to curl up in her own bed and sleep for days.

# Chapter 15

Emma sat next to Nate in the crowded ballroom. He held her hand and smiled down at her, beaming with pride. She had to admit, she was pretty-darn proud of herself. Three months had passed since she'd been rescued by this man, not once, but twice from a very determined terrorist. Her life had not been the same since. True to his word, Nate took her out on a real date. Dinner, a movie, and a night of making love that left her breathless. She laughed remembering her own words as he slowly stripped the wine-colored dress from her body.

"You know, I don't sleep with men on the first date." She'd offered him a cheeky smile while biting her lip. She knew that move drove him crazy. He'd said so many times.

Smiling wickedly, he'd nipped that inviting lip and growled, "That's good because you're not getting any sleep tonight, baby."

Although Nate had to report back to base in Fort Carson, he'd come up every weekend since, taking her on fun dates to include snowmobiling at a resort, wine-tasting in upstate New York followed by cozy nights by a fireplace whispering secrets and sharing histories. He'd gone into more detail about losing Charlie then. Seeing such vulnerability in a man as confident and strong as Nate melted her heart. It opened further when he'd shown up the third weekend with a very special present; a fluffy orange kitten wearing a green bowtie.

*"I went back and found him around the back of the safehouse. I figured since you risked your life for his, he deserved a second chance. Oh, and it's a 'he'. The vet said he's in good health and up to date on shots. They cleaned him up," he said, waiting for Emma to say something.*

*Her breath caught and her eyes welled up as a huge grin spread across her face. "Oh my gosh, Nate! He's precious." Emma took the kitten from his hands, cradling the fluff-ball to her chest.*

*The kitten sniffed her and then began to purr loudly.*

*"Oh, look, he remembers me!" She kissed his head and rubbed her chin on his fur.*

*Relieved that she liked his gift, Nate asked, "So what're you gonna name him?"*

*"Hmm, I don't know," she said, walking to the couch.*

*Nate followed. Together, they sat watching the little fellow reach for Emma's locket, pulling at it with his paw.*

*"I think maybe...Chance. Since we met by chance and we both got a second chance, I think it's fitting. What do you think?"*

*"I think it's perfect." He looked at her, intense emotions swirling in his blue eyes. "He's not the only one so lucky. You're my second chance, Emma."*

She blushed remembering that night. Her heart pounded with happiness. She had Chance, and she had Nate, and tonight, she was being honored as one of five recipients of the prestigious Goldsmith Investigative Journalism Awards. Her recent articles recounting her experience with Black Jihad's now deceased leader juxtaposed with her previous position on border security and immigration had led to a policy change in Homeland Security which closed the loopholes that allowed al-Waleed to enter the country on a counterfeit passport.

But more so than the recognition by her fellow journalists, she was touched by Nate's words. After the last article in the series published, he'd called her from Fort Carson.

*"I just finished reading your article. Emma, I'm so proud of you. Do you even know how amazing you are? Not many people could go through what you did and come out the other side with as much wisdom and compassion. You're a miracle. You're my miracle."*

She hadn't known what to say, but she'd basked in the glow of those words for a full week before his next visit that weekend, and then, she'd shown him just how much it meant to her—all night long.

When she'd been notified she was to be one of five recipients of the Goldsmith Award, the first person she called was Nate. Now, he was sitting by her side, her shiny award and a ten-thousand-dollar check between them, following the recognition ceremony. Despite that, all she could think of was being alone with her man. And the look he was giving her confirmed he was thinking the exact same thing.

"What are you thinking," she asked, knowing the answer.

"I'm thinking you've had one helluva thirtieth birthday, Miss Lewis."

This surprised her. "I guess so. I mean, it could've been my last, but then you rescued me, twice, and we began dating," she grinned, "and you gave me a kitten."

"And you've achieved outstanding recognition in your field," he said, pointing at her award.

"Oh, yes. There's that." She bit her lip, sliding her fingers through his. A secretive smile touched her lips. "Next year's birthday is going to seem downright boring compared to this one. Whatever will we do?"

Nate leaned over, dropping a soft kiss on her lips. "I actually had a thought or two about that," he said.

He pulled away, and stood, taking her hands.

Emma laughed, looking up at Nate. "Oh yeah, what?"

He dropped down to one knee and reached into his jacket withdrawing a small, blue box.

Emma's heart stopped, and she looked around. The people sitting at neighboring tables noticed and tapped their partners on the shoulder, pointing at Nate and Emma.

"Emma Jane Lewis, since I met you, my life has been turned inside-out...in the best possible way. I didn't even know how lonely my world had become until you smiled at me. Your warmth has healed my broken heart. You challenge me and defy me, and God help me, I love it. And how you forgave me even when my very existence put yours in danger is a mystery, but you did. You accept me with all my flaws without blinking an eye, and you understand me better than anyone ever has. I can't imagine my life without you. I don't want to. I want to share each day with you, talk to you, argue with you, laugh with you, spend each night loving you, and every morning waking up by your side. Emma, I've fallen so deeply in love with you." He paused, drawing a deep breath and then opened the box revealing a pear-shaped diamond set in platinum. "Will you marry me?"

Emma choked back a sob. Happiness burst within her like a supernova radiating out through tears of joy. "Yes, Nate. Yes, I will marry you, Nathan James Oliver!"

Relief shot through Nate. "You will?" Despite all his hope, he was still surprised. He looked at the people around them, all watching with smiles on their faces. "She said yes!"

Their applause filled his ears.

Leaping to his feet, he grabbed Emma around her waist, lifting her in the air and spun them both around. "I love you, Emma, so much!"

"I love you, too, Nate," she said, her arms wound tightly around his neck. "And I have a little surprise for you as well," she said, releasing him and stepping back. She reached down and placed her hands over her stomach.

Nate stared, unblinking, before letting out a loud whoop! "A baby?" We're having a baby?" "How did I ever get to be so lucky?"

Emma laughed as he lifted her up again, holding her tight as he whooped for joy before setting her down gently. "So, you're happy then because I wasn't sure..."

Nate kissed her. He put everything into that kiss. The crowd around them went wild, applauding and whistling. When he pulled away, he touched her face. "I'm so damned happy I feel like I could burst. Don't you ever doubt for a minute how happy I am, Emma. I promise I'm going to spend every day for the rest of our lives proving that to you." He kissed her again, quickly this time, before saying, "You know, it could've been Doc."

"What?" Emma blinked. "What could've been Doc?"

"He was going after you both that night, you and Becky. Well, because I put the kibosh on Ghost's attempted run at you, but that was because of the general's granddaughter," he rambled.

That surprised her. "So how is it he never got the chance?" she asked, laughing.

Nate pulled her close. "Because I wasn't about to let him get that close to you, the pervert. I knew I wanted you then. I know I want you now." His heated words were spoken against her lips.

"Thank goodness. I like Doc, but..."

"Don't even go there. Don't even think about that dimpled bastard. He's not allowed near you."

She slid her arms around his neck, caressing his hair. "But Allen might be a nice back-up, just in case..."

"Emma," Nate growled.

Emma giggled. "I'm pretty sure you have nothing to worry about, Captain, especially with regard to Doc. He and Becky are meeting up next week."

"Good. Let him pester her. As long as it's not my girl."

Emma sighed, happy. "I am. I'm yours. And you're mine." Emma released his neck. "Speaking of, don't you think you should make it official?" She waggled her fingers at him.

"Oh, yes!" Nate pulled back and, taking the ring from the box, took Emma's hand. The sparkling engagement ring slid onto her finger with ease. Nate lifted her hand and kissed it.

Emma stared into his blue eyes, again wondering what crazy twist of fate had brought this incredible, sweet, aggravating, amazingly sexy man into her life. He was everything she used to say she didn't want. How wrong she'd been. And thank goodness the universe hadn't listened. In that moment, all was right in the world, and she was happy.

As they basked in the moment, the blue of Nate's eyes intensified. She knew what that meant, and she grinned, biting her lip.

Nate groaned. "You ready to go home, soon-to-be Mrs. Oliver?"

Emma's heart skipped a beat hearing him address her as his missus. "Mine or yours?" she asked.

Nate pulled her close. "Ours."

"Oh." Emma blushed. "Yes, I'm ready, Captain Oliver."

Together, the happy couple left the crowded ballroom amid well-wishes from the men who clapped Nate on the back, and envious, but knowing looks from the wives. Emma knew her life would never be the same again...in the best possible way.

# Also By Michele E. Gwynn

Visit micheleegwynnauthor.com

<u>Green Beret Series</u>

*Rescuing Emma*

*Loving Leisl*

*Freeing Fatima*

*Saving Christmas*

*Loving Freddie*

*Saving Major Morgan (A prequel Novella)*

<u>The Soldiers of PATCH-COM</u>

*Secondhand Soldier*

*Second Chance Soldier*

*Second Breath Soldier*

*Silent Night Soldier*
*C'est la Vie Soldier (Coming Spring 2023)*

## The Checkpoint, Berlin Detective Series

*Exposed: The Education of Sarah Brown*
*The Evolution of Elsa Kreiss*
*The Redemption of Joseph Heinz*
*The Making of Herman Faust*

## The Harvest Trilogy

*Harvest*
*Hybrids*
*Census*

## SECTION 5 Series

*SECTION 5*

## Angelic Hosts Series

*Camael's Gift*
*Camael's Battle*
*Sophie's Wish*
*Nephilim Rising*

## Stand Alones

*Darkest Communion (Paranormal Romance)*
*Waiting a Lifetime (Contemporary Romance, Mystical)*
*Hiring John (Romantic Comedy)*

## Books by Michele E. Gwynn under Pen Names

*The Ascension of Dyonara by E.J. Lewis (Sci-Fi Reverse-Harem Romance)*

## Children's Fiction by M.E. Gwynn

*The Cat Who Wanted to be a Reindeer*
*The Humble Bumble Bee*
*Dirty Turtle Needs a Bath*

# Get a Free Book

*From the world of New York Times Bestselling Author Barry Eisler comes a fan fiction novella, John Rain: A Cell in San Antonio by Bestselling Author Michele E. Gwynn*

John Rain has 24 hours to repay a favor...the only way he knows how!

On the run from the Yakuza, Rain reluctantly takes a detour to the Alamo City to take out the son of the leader of an up and coming Mexican drug cartel. The Hands of Death have invaded yakuza territory, and their product is making a killing and endangering the unspoken understanding and often criminal alliance between the yakuza and Japanese government officials.

Juan Narvaez Morales, Jr. is in federal custody. The FBI seek to flip him as an asset but have only 72 hours in which to do so. On his last day in custody, Rain must successfully infiltrate the jail and terminate his target, all within 24 hours, and still make it out alive and undiscovered. This is a fast-paced thriller that will leave you on edge, and as always, cheering for John Rain.